PARABLES FROM PARADISE

A Selection of Dreams and Magical Tales

Written by Zacharias Topelius

Translated from the Swedish by Paul Gustav Whittaker

Printed and bound in Great Britain by:
Book Printing UK Remus House, Coltsfoot Drive, Woodston, Peterborough PE2 9BF

Published in the United Kingdom by
Imaginary Friends Publishing, Liverpool, L19 9EA

ISBN: 978-1-3999-9278-7

Acknowledgments
Editorial assistance from Kathleen Torbit and Helena Whittaker

Dedicated to the sisters Marianne (Bibbe) and Margareta (Pia)

Contents

Preface

Why read the tales of Topelius in his Reading for Children series? Once very popular in Finland, today the stories and their values and ideas may seem old-fashioned. However, I believe we can interpret his stories to give them relevance to contemporary life!

He does have a clear Christian focus. Religious beliefs and practices are occasionally mentioned, but you can decide what 'God' means to the characters, and to yourself. In fact, it is rare that 'God' takes an active part in these stories (see 'Christmas with the Trolls'). In contrast, a more common aspect of Topelius's stories is his inclusion of pagan themes. In 'Little Lasse' and 'Forest Bear', the boys' prayers to God are intercepted by the Sandman, who protects the children. In 'The Feather Isles', this Sandman (Nukku Matti, described as the elder brother of Death) is active in the Garden of Eden but has no religious role. In 'Sampo Lappelill' the eponymous hero struggles with the 'mountain king'. The Sámi fear this goblin and the trolls as much as they fear the wolves. The story 'The Water Nymph's Silver Bowl' describes the profound impact of a magical object (a familiar theme in Finnish legends and other folktales).

Let me give you some examples of stories that can be interpreted as quite modern. 'The Water Nymph's Silver Bowl' describes initiation and repression of adolescent sexual awareness, decades before Freud became popular. 'The Weathercock' illustrates the protagonist's hubris and eventual downfall which could easily describe the trajectory of many current politicians. 'The Old Cottage' comments on the fashion for turning the countryside into a replica of the city – quite a modern problem! Furthermore, in our more secular society, if we bear in mind that Christianity informed the moral education of children in 19th Century Finland and beyond, we can focus on the modern meaning of the stories' ethical messages. Qualities which he promotes, such as humility and concern for others, are still valuable in our modern age.

A prominent and attractive feature of Topelius's tales are descriptions and interactions with Nature, as well as a concern for the poor. Most importantly, the stories are well crafted and engaging; the storylines keep your attention by taking unexpected and dramatic turns. You want to read them to the end to find out what happens. So, read on!

Paul Whittaker,

Pennsylvania, 2022

The Weathercock

Once upon a time, a weathercock was sitting on top of a very tall church tower. Where he came from and how he got so high up in the world, it's not easy to say. Some believed that his father was not a regular rooster, but a carpenter who could carve out eagles and dragons from wood. People said that the carpenter cut the rooster out of a log and hoisted him up onto the tower, but because the rooster was so wooden, he could not learn to fly.

Maybe that wasn't so; perhaps the rooster was previously the finest cockerel in the henhouse of the mighty Fairie Queen[1]. In his pride, he had rebelled against his ruler; his punishment was to be transformed into a wooden cockerel and nailed to the tower. Nobody really knows for sure.

Anyway, he sat on the tower at the very top, well above the highest roof and the highest tree for seven miles around. And he sat so high up that the whole world around him did not look much bigger than a pancake, and the people looked like flies on the pancake. The rooster saw them buzzing awhile, and he saw them chased away, as if by a big flyswatter.

The church rooster was exceptionally large. He had a tall, red-painted cockscomb above his beak, green eyes as big as plates, and a very bushy tail. He was so puffed-up that his stomach had enough room for three bushels of barley. He thought that because he was so big and sat up so high, no one in the whole world was such a fine gentleman as he was.

All roosters are proud; one can see it in their manners, bragging on the rubbish-heap with their beak in the air, as if they wanted to shout to everybody: 'What kind of rascal are you?' But the church rooster was one of the worst. Such an attitude never ends well. Many a grand, audacious rooster has lost his neck when his owners prepared a feast, and then unceremoniously he has been plucked, laid in the stewpot and eaten like any other poultry, with gravy, gherkins and lingonberry jam.

Perhaps the weathercock knew that he was not tasty enough to be beheaded and eaten, and this made him more conceited than other roosters. He had the habit, quite common here in the world, of constantly turning his tail according to the weather. Therefore, he could look around in all directions. But wherever he looked with his big green eyes, nowhere on earth did he see his equal. He therefore began to believe he was much better than everyone else and that the whole world should be subservient to him. That's why he thought to himself:

'I'm a grand rooster, a very noble and handsome cockerel am I. Without any peer, I'm the real rooster king. It is obvious that the church was built solely for my sake, to provide for me a place worthy of my high rank. Why would the people gather here every Sunday around the church, if not to admire and worship me? Yes, it is certain I'm a magnificent rooster, a most distinguished and worthy one.'

But noble folk sometimes experience boredom, and so it was with the weathercock. He couldn't fly, he wouldn't work and didn't need to eat. What should he do? Sometimes, with a certain envy, he watched the parson's chickens, as they came up to the base of the tower and scratched up the sand to collect a few grains of corn.

One day it happened that a crow flew over the church, quite close to the weathercock, who sat there irritated and annoyed that someone had presumed to fly almost as high up as his perch.

"Craw! craw!" shrieked the crow. "How are you doing, dear cockerel?"

"Grrr!" said the cockerel, spun around by the wind and with his tail turned to the crow. "I think you could at least call me 'Excellency'."

"Look at that!" said the crow. "Well, isn't your 'Excellency' deadly dull, to sit there all alone and do nothing. I think your 'Excellency' should get married."

"Get married?" said the cockerel. "Where would I find a hen, elevated and ladylike, that I could attach myself to without harm to my rank?"

"Your 'Excellency' is correct," replied the crow, "such a hen is not easy to find. I don't remember that I ever heard of ecclesiastical hens. But your 'Excellency' could at least take on some work. That's what I do; it passes the time and makes the spirit happy and cheerful."

"Work!" The cockerel spun around and looked at the crow with deep contempt. "Grand and distinguished folk usually never work. It just wouldn't do."

'Ha, ha,' thought the crow to herself, as she flew away. 'You look all around you and still know so little about how the world works. I have often noticed that the high and noble have more work and more worries than the low and humble in this world. But such dumb bigshots like you think gentility consists of sitting idly by and doing nothing to make Creation grand. Let others get past you and have their hearts broken. It is also obvious that the weathercock is hundreds of years old and thinks like so many others did in his youth. But now we understand better than before that everyone must work and be diligent if they want to be happy and satisfied. The weathercock doesn't understand this. Because he's so bone-idle, he says: 'It just wouldn't do'.

And that's how it really was. The rooster was lazy and arrogant, that was all. For several hundred years, he had sat there on the spire-tip and not done a thing; he hadn't crowed once. Yes, he was so lazy, he hadn't budged at all in hundreds of years; how lazy is that?

One fine day, when the weathercock was sitting as usual, staring out into the blue sky and looking particularly important, not thinking of anything, he was amazed to see a large crowd of people in front of the church.

'What can it be?' he thought, 'today is not Sunday.' Soon enough, he got to see what it was.

It was the great tightrope walker Karamatti, who had tied a rope between the church tower and the belfry. On the rope, a little boy and a little girl jumped and danced together and made marvellous turnabouts.

'Oh,' thought the rooster, 'it is nothing special. I thought there was some new ceremony that the stupid people were celebrating here in my honour.'

Just then, the little Karamatti threw a kiss to the people, and he climbed like a cat up the church tower, up the old iron rungs set into the spire. Higher and higher, the little Karamatti climbed until finally, he was close to the rooster.

'Aha,' thought the rooster, and looked infuriated.

But Karamatti was not frightened, and with a hop, skip and a jump, he sprang onto the rooster's back, sat astride it and screamed with all his might:

"Whoo-hoo, my horsey! Hi-yo, my fine steed!"

You can imagine that the conceited rooster became wide-eyed, up until now supposing that no one in the world was his equal. And now there sat a little lad who rode on him and shouted:

"Whoo-hoo, my horsey! Hi-yo, my pretty pony!"

At first, the rooster expected the whole church would topple in awe at such impertinence. But the church stood quietly calm where it was, and now the cockerel, in his great humiliation, began to twist and turn in all directions. What could he do? He had been so lazy that he had neither learned how to fly nor to crow; therefore, he had to put up with all the people below calling out: "Bravo! Bravissimo!" and reckoning it was very clever of little Karamatti to ride on the weathercock. Yes, that's how it goes in the real world: when someone is lazy and stuck-up, along comes a little Karamatti and rides on him, as he rode on the weathercock. Be sure of it.

But the rooster hadn't learnt this lesson. He remained on the top of the spire year after year, while one generation after another sang hymns to the glory of God in the church below, lived out their time and then went to the grave, and new people came in their stead and sang the same old hymns in the same old church. All the while, the rooster sat there, still as lazy and as high and mighty as ever, expecting that eventually, by some wonderful blessing, he would be rewarded for his great nobility. Maybe he stood waiting to be gilded with the brightest gold and shine like the sun, or he expected one day to be proclaimed throughout the world as a grand Sultan rooster. Oh, who can know for certain?

He waited and waited, and that great reward never came. He waited so long, becoming incredibly old and rotten, that one piece after another fell off him when the wind blew. One day there was a strong storm. A gust of wind came whistling over the church, blew the cockerel off from the steeple and carried him through the air to the lake. There the rooster landed, giddy from his unusual journey and forever after regretful that he had not learned to fly and crow. For if he could have, he would not have blown into the lake, but instead flown to the town hall roof and sat crowing there, so that the magistrate and the whole town would hear him. But now he fell into the lake and was thrown back and forth by the waves, so that the pike and the perch gaped at him and wondered what kind of water-spirit he was. Eventually, he was thrown up onto a beach, and there he lay.

By the shore was a small cottage, and there lived a young woman who had two children, a boy and a girl. The children were building small pools on the beach, safe harbours for the small fish, which swam in and out. When they went a little farther afield to look for stones, they found the poor old weathercock, and he looked pretty wretched. The waves had completely washed away his painted decoration, and he'd been bashed against the rocks, losing both beak and tail.

Then the children said: "Look here, we're in luck; Mother always complains that crows and sparrows damage the vegetable patch. We've found a nice scarecrow. Come, let us take a rope and haul him up to the pea bed."

And so, the weathercock spent his later days set up on a fence post to scare crows away from a pea bed, instead of being gilded and proclaimed throughout the world as a grand Sultan rooster. Then one day the crow, who in the rooster's better days had called him your 'Excellency', came flying in to have a feast in the pea bed. Uh-oh - she saw the scarecrow and flew away. But during her escape, she looked back and saw he was familiar.

"Craw! craw!" screeched the crow. "I do believe I have the honour of addressing his 'Excellency', who has now become a scarecrow. Well, well, vanity, vanity, that's how the world turns."

"Hold your beak!" squawked a wise raven, sitting on a pine stump nearby. "The rooster has been arrogant and lazy, and therefore it has gone badly for him. But now he's old and miserable, and one shouldn't scorn those who are elderly and unhappy. No one can know how their own life may turn for good or ill in their later days."

The weathercock heard all this. But he could not say a word, because he was without a beak and sat strung up on a fence post. He probably still sits there today.

The Old Cottage

Away at the northern end of the island, there at the top of the hill, looking out over the treetops and the blue waves, stood a very old cottage, so old that no one could say when it was built. Unpainted and roughly hewn, the half-rotted logs looked as if they would fall out of the walls, and in the windows there were no unbroken panes, just a shard of glass here and there. The chimney had long since fallen, and if the fireplace inside had not collapsed, it was only because it had been strongly constructed of large, grey stones, which defied decay. The floor was full of big holes, gnawed by rats hoping to pilfer something good from the hut, and overall, it appeared quite dusty and black and chaotic in the deserted building.

But far away in the darkest corner, half behind a high wall-mounted bed that reached up to the ceiling, something beautiful and brilliant glittered. Could it have been silver or gold, or a precious stone? Maybe it was the bright glint of the evening sun which crept through a crevice, its beauty contrasting against the darkness of the cottage. Perhaps it was a dragon's fiery breath that burned over hidden treasure, or possibly an old tomte[1], lighting his pipe in the quiet of the evening?

No, shall I tell you what it was? It was neither gold nor silver, nor sun, nor ghosts; it was only a piece of an old log in the wall. Due to age and dampness, it had become completely rotten, and now it shone in the dark, as old timber sometimes does. That was all it was.

Then again, I have my own thoughts about it. I think that all the beautiful memories, all the happy thoughts, all the jokes, the happiness and pleasures, which in times past thrived within the walls of this cottage, lived on in its darkest corners and shone there as a happy recollection of the past. I think that the old pine in the wall glistened with joy in remembrance, and that was the reason why it shone.

For if you knew everything this cottage had seen in its day, you would think like me. It had been the only house on the whole beautiful island, and its door was never closed. It stood open to the poor and the rich, for those sad or happy. It offered them all a welcome shelter from the storms, a roof when it rained, a stove to cook the lively perch[2], and a bed of the softest hay when the evening came and repose was sweet. All summer, one saw happy people here from the city and the whole district. They lived here without ceremony or much fuss, they cooked coffee together in the large shiny copper kettle, they played their games, and they slept side by side in a bed of straw on the floor while those better off or elderly slept in proper beds of hay, only the nobility slept on eiderdown.

And all the joking and amusements, all those embarrassments, the hilarious antics and fun events that this cabin had witnessed - no, they would be impossible to describe. Now it stood deserted and derelict and of all its former inhabitants there was only one family which did not abandon the cottage in its old age; that was the mosquitoes. In times past they were not very welcome when the cottage was inhabited by people who loved a good night's rest; residents used to lay large juniper twigs in the fireplace and put a cap on the chimney so that the cottage became full of smoke; this greatly deterred the mosquitoes. But now they were undisturbed, dancing their quadrilles in the sunshine around the broken windows; they did not get to feast on young human blood but at least they were safe from juniper smoke. When the mosquitoes now living boasted of being the descendants of the mosquitoes which had their haunt in the old cottage during happier times, they retained a certain fondness for the place, and still felt at home there even though their only food consisted of sunshine and summer wind.

Why had the old cottage had been abandoned? In more modern times, people preferred to spend the summer in the newer, and much better furnished, dwellings built up all over the island. These new houses were really like small palaces with two floors and all the amenities that one could imagine; in their neighbourhood one saw gardens with proper paths and flower beds, and if you wanted to talk politely and please the owner, you could ask him how it was possible to build such a beautiful villa in the wild forest, by the rough sea. Then the owner of the villa would nod and inform you: hmm, when you get painters and gardeners and a whole gang of other artisans from the city, chop down the wild trees and cut and trim and spend a few thousand Finnmarks, then surely at last the impossible will become possible.

The new villas had beautiful names, such as Lisedal, Sanssouci and Framnäs. People lived there just like in the city, received visitors and had musical soirees; one could see green game tables, along with skittle alleys and merry-go-rounds. When people went out for a walk, then it was on sandy paths and green painted Chinese bridges over the narrow streams, but they only went occasionally into the green fragrant forest, when the arctic brambles[3] shone crimson amongst the tussocks and the wild strawberries beckoned invitingly on the steep slopes. Young women then hitched up their skirts, took small, neat baskets in their hands and went out for an hour or two on adventures.

In one of the most handsome villas, which bore the stately name Albano, two girls, Antonia and Marie, lived with their parents. They were both young, beautiful and happy, both exuberant and carefree, but in different ways; so that while Antonia, with all her young heart's desire, was bound to the pleasures of the day and the joy of the moment, Marie had a deeper spirit, open to all impressions; and that was why she could be so much happier, because she could also be sad sometimes.

Besides the parents, the siblings and the whole household, who had now moved out there for the summer, the old grandmother also lived there in her own little chamber up on the second floor. She was nearly ninety and completely blind, and she knew and remembered little of what was going on, but like many of the elderly back then, she knew some books by heart. She sat there singing hymns without assistance; every morning all the children came in line and kissed the old lady on the hand and smiled among themselves when she asked them their names for the hundredth time.

Of all the children, Marie was the one who kept close to her old grandmother and the only one whose name the old woman did not forget. For that reason, she was jokingly called little Grandma by the others: 'because you are so like old Grandma in her chair,' they said. And although Marie loved her grandmother, she couldn't help but notice the many wrinkles and the grey, withered skin on the old woman's cheeks; and when the others said, 'You are so like Grandma!' she wept. The ninety-year-old heard this, where she sat, and she said consolingly: "Don't cry, Maja dear; you should see my portrait!"

For at home in the city, in the large, impressive drawing room, two old paintings in oval gilded frames hung on the wall. There was a young man of thirty years in a powdered wig with a pigtail, a dress coat with big shiny buttons, fine cuffs and a splendid ruff with lace; and by his side in the other painting there was a young, beautiful and happy wife, twenty years of age, with swept-up hair, a blouse with a long, tight-fitting bodice and a flowery stiff gown. The year 1775 appeared on both paintings. They were grandfather and grandmother's portraits, painted in Stockholm, when they were newly married. Grandfather was dead long ago, but the young beautiful lady with the haughty smile and yet so good-natured an appearance, with pretty dimples in her fine, blossoming cheeks and the tender sweet shine of her blue eyes, was the same blind, ninety-year-old woman who sat there with the many wrinkles on her cheek, with grey skin and withered hands in her solitary chamber - yes, it was old grandmother seventy years ago. She was still thinking of her youth's happy days, when she had heard so many flattering words about her beautiful appearance, and so she said quietly and kindly, without a single bitter thought about the impermanence of all earthly beauty: "Don't cry, Maja dear; you should see my portrait!"

One morning the sun rose up red over the sea and as large as a wagon wheel, and that day it became quite warm. Antonia and Marie took their baskets and went out to pick brambles. It was so beautiful, so still, in the groves of birch and alder and their shade was so wonderfully cool. The large dark red berries gleamed under dense leaves at the edge of the tussocks; the girls had never picked such swollen, ripe and juicy berries. The more they explored the deciduous forest and the fragrant, still uncut, meadows, the more berries they found, and the faster they filled their baskets. It was delightful fun, and so they continued picking until well into the afternoon.

"Now it may be time to go home again, because the sun is starting to burn as hot as a baker's oven," said Antonia.

"Just wait a little," said Marie. "I only need twenty more berries to have a full basket." And so they went even further across the long grass.

"I have never been this far before," said Antonia. "Do you see the old ramshackle cottage there between the trees? It looks like a tomte's mansion. Do you think that trolls are even allowed to live on our beautiful island?"

"The cottage is ugly and old!" replied Marie. "But it is not right that we despise it for its old age. Grandma is also ugly and old, but she is nevertheless so kind and was so beautiful when she was young."

"You are talking about such an old ruin!" Antonia laughed.

"But now we should go home, because it is my turn to serve the tea tonight."

"You say that, but which way should we go?"

"Come with me here to the left."

"You're mistaken, it's towards the right."

"We came from over here."

"But before that we went all the time to the left. You know, Marie, we are lost."

"I'm thinking the same thing, Antonia."

"What should we do now?"

"We should walk along the seashore and then we would finally arrive back at Albano."

"Yes, tomorrow! Don't you know that the island is miles in circumference?"

"Oh, that's awful. And now it is starting to rain."

"Ugh, a really black cloud is moving over the sun; there will be a terrible storm."

"The sky is rumbling …"

"Did you see the lightning ... Antonia!"

"The drops are falling as big as cherries."

"Our new dresses!"

And the two girls started running as fast as they could, without knowing for sure where they were going. The rain fell more fiercely, lightning kept flashing; the thunder rolled through the clouds with a sharp and ringing boom, as if a heavy wagon were rumbling down a cobbled street in a great hurry. It was an awful storm.

"Now I can't go any further," said Antonia, drenched, exhausted and pale with fright.

"Let's rest here under this tall birch," said Marie.

"No, no, certainly not! Haven't you heard that lightning often strikes tall trees?"

"That's true! We have to run even further."

And so they ran. But after a while they were back in the same place where they had begun.

Now the poor girls became anxious, Antonia grabbed a tree trunk and said, "Now I am going no further, even if the thunderstorm hits me."

Marie began to cry.

But at that moment, the heavy clouds lightened, and the girls saw the half-derelict wall of the old cottage quite close to them on the hill.

"Come sister," Marie shouted, and in less than two minutes, both were under cover.

Why would Antonia be so scornful about the poor, battered building? It looked messy, it is true, and in comparison to Albano there was much to criticize. But they had found a hospitable shelter from the storm, and if you didn't get too close to the corners, where the rain dripped in through the broken roof, then you could be sitting quite safe and secure.

"Here we feel like pearls," laughed Marie, who was always easily satisfied. "You see, the tomte has been expecting guests. Why else would he have spread fresh birch-leaves all over the floor and put fresh, fragrant hay in the beds? Let the rain and lightning come: the cottage has endured many storms in its time."

"Fishermen have been here today," Antonia remarked, "and they'll be back soon. They have left a frying pan on the stove, and over there I see the head of a perch."

"Ah, if only we had a little fire to dry our clothes!"

"Let see! Well, there are embers glowing in the ash."

"Blow, Antonia, pooof! Once again, pooof! Now it's catching fire and the shavings are burning beautifully! Here, lay pieces of that old dry alder on it, and we will get a nice fire. Another piece of wood ... now then, I said that we would begin to feel like pearls!"

While Marie was speaking that way to cheer her sister up, she had managed to get a good fire blazing. The old alder crackled and sparkled as it was burning, and in a while both girls' clothes were almost dry. Now they wanted to try to find their way home again, but the rain was torrential; it was impossible to go out in such weather along the confusing paths through the high grass. They must wait then, and the passing of time would be slow and tedious. They decided to examine the cottage more closely; who knows what they could discover?

On the old smoky and dusty walls, Antonia found several verses written, some tender, some comic, which she declaimed with hilarious solemnity! One read as follows:

'Lovely girl, I keep repeating your name!

I follow you like your own shadow.'

And underneath, a roguish wit had written:

'If I could right now, I would pull your hair.'

Another verse read:

Once I was in Arcadia,

Now I have returned there.'

"Oh, so tender and moving!" exclaimed Antonia.

But there was an even more emotional verse:

'Farewell! Don't forget me!

How life's destiny is dawning,

For you, for you, I breathe,

Beate Sophie, for you'

"Beate Sophie, those are Grandma's first names!" exclaimed Marie.

"There may well have been many others named Beate Sophie, not just Grandma," Antonia replied and continued to recite phrases from the walls. But in the end, it got dark, so she could not see anything anymore, and then both sisters sat down by the fireplace again.

"You know what?" sighed Marie.

"What then?" Antonia asked.

"We must stay here tonight. As the rain and lightning hasn't stopped yet, we can't go out and get lost in the forest at night."

"Ah yes!" sighed Antonia. "But I'm hungry."

"I have a remedy for that," replied Marie (she had ideas for everything). "I have read in a book, that the Arabs of the desert often make do with a handful of boiled rice for supper."

"We have juniper berries and crowberries." Antonia laughed. "Which one do you intend to cook soup with?"

"Wait and see!" And then Marie picked up a handful of rice grains from her dress pocket, which she liked to eat dry, as girls are used to doing before growing up. Then she wiped a pan very clean, put it out in the rain, got some water in it and put the rice grains on to boil. In a while they were ready, and after she squeezed a little arctic bramble juice over the rice, it tasted excellent.

"You always get it right, don't you!" said Antonia.

Now the girls searched for the cleanest bed, in which there was perfectly dry hay, and lay there to rest after they had tried to close the door as best they could. Soon Antonia was fast asleep.

But Marie's eyes did not close. She thought about how worried their parents would be for the girls' safety; she thought of old Grandma, of the verses to Beate Sophie and a thousand other things which come to a young girl when she cannot sleep. She tried all the tricks she could to encourage sleep; she thought of the most unpleasant thing she knew, the old snuff-taking military official, who always wanted to kiss her with his toothless mouth; she counted from one to three hundred and thirty-three. Nothing helped.

Finally, she turned around. Then her gaze fell on the dark corner opposite. Something gleamed there as clear as fire, and yet the glow was whiter and paler than firelight. 'Is it really a glowing ember from the fireplace?' she thought.

She had to go and look. She got up; she went over. No, there was no firelight; it was nothing more than the old, half-decayed wood, which glowed in the dark. Marie looked at it for a moment with amusement. Then she noticed another small piece in the wall, which also shone, but with an even whiter glow. 'It is also rotten wood,' she thought, and put her hand on it. But no, it was a small ring, which sat deep in a crack in the wall. With difficulty she got it out and, though it was dark, she saw that the light came from a small diamond embedded in the ring. What a find! And how it had tried Marie's patience not to be able to look at the ring up close! She pressed it onto her finger and returned to the bed. Now sleep was not long in coming.

Surely you have heard of Dreamland[4]? There Marie was at home like all good children and the golden dreamchildren fluttered on sky-blue wings around her bed. They took her by the hand, they brought her seventy years back in time; there she saw her old grandmother at the age of seventeen, so happy, smiling, so kind-hearted and beautiful, like Marie herself … She sat there in the same old cottage where Marie now slept - but then you should have seen how the cottage was so white and new and beautiful! - and beside the seventeen-year-old grandmother stood a handsome boy of twenty years in a sailor's suit. They rinsed berries - they looked at each other ... What bright, friendly eyes! Were they Grandma's eyes? … Yes, yes, they were the same, but seventy years ago! Then the handsome blonde boy took her hand, kissed it, rushed out - and sailed in a ship away over the sea. Oh, how old grandmother wept … (I always say old grandmother; she was seventeen years old) … Oh, how she cried, the beautiful, sweet, young girl! Her brothers and sisters came to the cottage, all with baskets full of berries ... They made a ring around the old grandmother - around their beloved young sister, they danced around her, they wanted to console her and make her happy, but she was crying ... crying and looking towards the shiny, vanishing edge of the blue sea to the north!

Marie woke up and looked around. Gone was the young girl who was crying; gone was the boy, gone was the beautiful new cottage. At home in Albano, old grandmother sat ninety and blind and Marie lay in the dilapidated grey cottage which was threatening to collapse. It felt so strange in Marie's heart.

Nonetheless, she sank back into the friendly arms of dreams and now they brought her seventy years ahead in time. What did she see? Was this the island? How different, and yet how familiar! Gone was the old cottage, gone without a trace, without anyone now living on earth knowing it existed; only Marie knew, she alone. Where the cottage and the villas had once stood, and all over the formerly green island, now stretched streets and squares with tall buildings, rolling carriages and wagons, bustling with people rushing by. There was life, noise and movement, the city had expanded here from its former place on the mainland and had become four times as large, populous and prosperous … Ah, but where were the beautiful arctic brambles, the sweet songbirds in the solitary peace of the forest groves? They had fled from the noise; they did not thrive in the landscaped gardens, which were built all along the shore. Look there; there appeared a very old woman, surrounded by her great-grandchildren. Her feet were lame, she could no longer walk, she was carried in a chair; she was deaf, she could not hear, but she was not blind, like old grandmother. She looked so good, so amiable in her old age; who could she be? Marie saw her in the dream, looked at her carefully, loved her, kissed her hand, but did not know her … Then a voice whispered in her ear: 'it's you'; it was Marie seventy years from now! … Then Marie started in her sleep, it felt so strange around her heart again; she wanted to cry with both sorrow and love, but she could not … She felt so old, so old; she was the lame and deaf ninety-year-old woman, who sat there in the wheelchair … she looked back ... way back! She looked at the place where the old cottage had once stood and where now a small gazebo rose with bright red silk curtains and a small pennant on the roof. She said to her great-grandchildren: 'Can you believe that here once stood an old, dilapidated cabin full of so many, many memories? One hundred and forty years ago, my grandmother was standing here in the same place saying farewell to a cheerful boy, who went away to sea and never came back... and seventy years ago, when I was young and childish myself, my sister Antonia and I got lost in the forest. We slept overnight in the old cottage, and I found a ring there... I was seventeen then! ...' And one young girl, who seemed closest to the beautiful young Marie... no, what am I saying? … the ninety-year-old, withered, lame and deaf old woman! … the young girl looked up in surprise at the old woman in the wheelchair and said in her naive innocence: 'Is it possible that Grandma was also once seventeen years old?!'

Then it became tight again around Marie's heart, she saw a mist descend over the gazebo with the red silk curtains and the pennant on the roof, and the mist muddled everything, even the old woman in the wheelchair and the children chatting around her ... and Marie woke up and felt warm tears fall onto her cheeks. Frightened, she stood up ... Was she really as old and withered and decayed as she had just seen herself, there in the wheelchair? Oh no, she was as young, as light on her feet as before; her cheeks were fine, warm, soft and red, she looked at her hands, they were as white and soft as before! Yes, she was still seventeen, and what she had seen, and what had so wonderfully touched her heart and brought her to tears - it was all a dream!

Was it all a dream?

Yes, for now the sun was shining in so brightly through the broken windows of the old, grey cottage; the thunder and the rain had stopped, and lovely scents wafted in from the surrounding forest.

Marie moved her hand over her forehead. "It was a dream," she said softly to herself; but what a dream!

Antonia was still asleep. Marie woke her with a kiss, and then they hitched up their dresses, because the grass was still quite wet, and bid the cottage farewell. But they had not gone far before they saw a boat on the nearby shore, in which their worried father was sitting, who had rowed out to search for the lost children. In less than an hour they were at Albano again.

Antonia had much to recount when she returned home: about the thunderstorm, about the grubby old cottage and the ridiculous verses that were written on the cottage walls. But Marie went straight to the old grandmother, embraced her, kissed her withered hands, and covered her with caresses. She could not forget her dream, she kept thinking: 'such as I am, Grandma has also been; as Grandma is, so I will be too!' And then she thought of the handsome sailor, who went away to sea forever, and she was thinking of, I will not say who, and how wonderful that after seventy years she would think back to him and to all those sweet days of youth, which she was now playing out in joy. Then the tears rose again in Marie's gentle eyes; after all, they welled up constantly, she was so often sad or very happy, the little, good Marie.

"Can Grandma imagine?" she said, "I have been in the old cottage! There was Grandma's name on the wall, and all night long I dreamt of Grandma's strange affairs long ago."

But the old woman did not hear her; she just held Marie's hand in hers and looked attentively at the diamond ring, which sat on Marie's ring finger.

"The ring, the ring!" she said in a trembling voice. "Where did you find the ring?"

"I found it in the old cabin, deep in a crack in the wall."

"It's the same as my ring!" exclaimed the old woman. She bent down, kissed the ring, and pushed it onto her wrinkled finger. "Thank you, little Maja; it is the same one, yes, yes, the same! I looked for it yesterday; I searched the whole day and was not able to find it."

"Yesterday, Grandma? Yesterday?"

"Wasn't it yesterday? No, you are right, it was several weeks ago. It was when he went away."

"The handsome young sailor in the blue jersey?"

"Yes, that's him. Do you know him?"

"The young man who cleaned berries with Grandma in the old cottage and then went away to sea?"

"The same one, yes. You may not know that we loved each other a lot. We had loved each other since we were little; he was only three years older than me. He was like a brother to me, but he loved me more than one loves a sister. When he went away a few weeks ago, he told me: 'Beate Sophie, you don't love me the way I love you; I'm leaving now and may never come back. But here in the cottage I have hidden the ring you saw yesterday; seek it, it is yours! When you have the ring in your hand again, you will know that I will be back with you soon; but if you never find it, we will never see each other again.'"

"Did you look for the ring, Grandma?"

"I was always looking for it! Day and night, night and day, but I never found it. I searched for it summer after summer, and he never came back. Tell me, little Maja, maybe it has been a long time since he left? Maybe it's been several months?"

"Oh, Grandma ... that was seventy years ago!"

"Seventy years! ... Child, you are right, I had not thought about that. That day is like yesterday for me; everything in between has flowed past me like a river, and I have remained alone on the shore. Tell me, what is written there on the inside of the ring?"

"1772. I will come back to you!"

"He was coming back to me! Yes, now I know that he will not come to me, but rather I will come to him. He is in the bright spaces where there is no farewell. I will be there soon too. Then he will come to me!"

"No Grandma, you must not die and leave us!"

"Don't you grieve, little Maja! The long days turn to evening as well as the short ones. But whether the days have been short or long, in the end every hour brings us closer to God's kingdom. Then you meet the night with joy and rest in peace, the night passes away and becomes a blessed and eternal morning."

Thus did old Grandma speak, with such a heavenly faith as only they can have who have been tested a great deal and yet maintained their faith to the end. When next summer came, the thin, young grass was already green over her grave. Antonia and Marie went back to the island with their parents at the same time in August as the previous year.

"Come sister," said Marie, "let's see if the old cottage is still there!"

"Let's go," said Antonia, "but now we must definitely take notice of the way so that we do not get lost." And so they went.

When they arrived at the beautiful hill by the sea, the old cottage was no more; it had collapsed the previous November during the autumn storms. Some of the logs had been dragged away; other timbers, which were the most rotten, were still standing, along with a large heap of grey stone where the girls had cooked rice porridge. Only the mosquitoes danced, as before, over the small ruin, and the setting sun cast its gentle rays of gold over the fading memories of the wrecked dwelling.

"What do I see!" exclaimed Antonia. "The tomte is homeless, his castle has fallen, and now he may be moving his home to Albano!"

Marie did not hear her. She looked at the desolate remains of the cottage, gilded by the sun as if there was hope of a future, and she said softly to herself: "In seventy years, a large city with ships and factories will have grown up around here and at this place a small gazebo will stand with pennants at the top and bright red side curtains. Then no one will remember that there was an old cottage here, where good, happy people lived ... an old woman is the only one who will remember it ..."

"Come, Marie, come!" shouted Antonia. "The most beautiful, reddest, sweetest brambles are growing here. See how they glisten! How good they smell! Oh, to me, nothing on earth is more delicious than really large, clear, dark red arctic brambles. Don't you agree?

"Ah, yes, yes, let's pick them!" Marie said and smiled. And in that childish, sweet, innocent smile, both the past and the future vanished.

The Feather Isles

Far out in the Gulf of Bothnia, midway between Sweden and Finland, there are some small green islands called the Feather Isles. As you sail out on the endless sea, where the waves grow as high as houses and ships perish on autumn nights, you would never imagine that such islands could offer a wholesome, friendly port to the weary sailor. No storm blows there, no high waves heave, no lone seagull raises its monotonous cry over the foaming surf. Everything breathes a wonderful calm. The wind rests, the waves sleep, the birds sing softly and slowly, and the moonlight shines with a golden glow over the trees and fragrant flowers which drink the clear dew in the cool of the evening.

For those who wrestle with the ocean waves of life in their small dinghy, it is wonderful to finally be able to rest on such benevolent shores as the Feather Isles. Many seek them in vain, are thrown by the waves night and day and never find the Feather Isles. Quite a few would give gold and green forests if they could find these blessed islands, and yet they sink deep, deep, deep into the sea.

There is something unique and mysterious about these Feather Isles. There is no helmsman so confident and knowledgeable, even if he has sailed around the world, who can find the Feather Isles in broad daylight. But if, tired from work and vigil, he makes his prayers devoutly, if he lies down quietly in his dinghy and lets the slow current move where it wants, then he will get there as surely as if he steered by compass and nautical charts. For you come to the Feather Isles through unfathomable waterways which are not marked on any nautical chart.

Those who have worked hard with a good conscience, whether in good health or sick and afflicted, will find their tranquil harbour. And then they forget all their pains; then they relax as happily as good children leaning against their mother's bosom.

This may seem very strange, and perhaps you think that these islands do not exist at all. But they are as certain as the sun, which goes down in the evening and rises again every morning over both good and evil. Ask all good children: they probably know the Feather Isles. It is impossible to pinpoint the location of the Feather Isles because every morning, when the rooster crows, they sink with all their glory down into the depths of the sea, and every evening, when the shadows grow long and the stars begin to twinkle in the sky, these sea secrets, with all their greenery, rise again from the depths. Then they float, light as down and feathers, on the shiny surface of the sea; maybe that is how they got their name.

On these delightful islands, in the middle of the deepest forest, where everything is quiet, sacred, and mysterious, there is a cave, built of shells and adorned with all the splendour of the earth, all the glory of the evening sky and all the riches of the sea. There the bluest stars twinkle, there the most precious stones shine. On stairs of precious coral, the wanderer descends into halls of mother of pearl, where walls of brightest gold are reflected in floors of shiny silver and ceilings of radiant crystal. A million genuine pearls sit like countless small windows fitted into the gold walls, and sparkling diamonds hang like flames down from the ceiling. All the summer's beloved flowers fill these halls with their delicate perfume. A gentle numbness, a quiet peace descends upon those who inhale their fragrance. But the strongest scent of all the flowers is from the common and insignificant poppy. From the dark red and black-green flower crown spreads a pleasant but stupefying vapor, sweeter than the sweetest honey.

Many hundreds, even countless halls are in this beautiful cave. They are all high and radiant, but their light is not the white light of day, it is like starlight and moonlight over a beautiful lake at night. Therefore, when you enter the halls from the dazzling sunshine, you first seem to enter a wonderful world of shadows and twilight. But soon you notice how all objects shimmer in their own marvellous lustre without ever dazzling.

And in this gentle light, one clearly discerns and recognizes all the beloved features of one's dear old acquaintances. There your best friends will come to you, just as if they were at home there, and take you in their arms and make you warmly welcome. Yes, even though they are far away at the end of the world, even though they are dead in eternal peace and you cried a thousand tears on their green graves, yet they will meet you here in these beautiful caves, flourishing with health and youth, so happy, so blessed, as if sorrow and death had never separated you. You take them by the hand, you kiss their rosy cheeks, and you think that everything is as before. Then you play the old childhood games again. The splendid ball, which you got when you were little and which has long been lost, God knows where, you will find it again, it flies like before and no ball in the world flies like it. And the dear old doll, which long ago lost both head and arms; and the painted wooden horse, which you once received as a Christmas present, but eventually all four legs broke off; and the beautiful picture book, that your little sister tore up the time you were away; and the toboggan with iron under the runners, the one which raced past all the other sleds and you mourned so much when it was stolen - you will find them all again, new, beautiful, just like before. The ball is spotless; the doll is whole and stylish in her first new outfit; the horse has its four proper legs; the picture book is undamaged, not even dog-eared, and the sled desires nothing better than to be able to take up speed again on the hill. Yes, who could believe such happiness? But you accept the wonderment.

Now you want to play. But it does not really work that way, as with other games. A toy disappears from your hands, and you do not know how; immediately you hold another in your hand, and you have not taken it, it has laid itself there. Your friends come and go in the same wonderful way. You yourself are here and there, in much haste, but never arriving. You travel like magic through the air. Just as you are playing in your old home, where everything is so well known, in the same moment you have had time to read your schoolwork in the classroom and do not know how you got there. And just when you are sitting in your boat on the lake and have rowed several miles with a single stroke of the oars, you have at the same moment climbed up to the top of a high mountain. But this does not upset you in the slightest. The dog that barked at you yesterday has suddenly become the same dog that many years ago ran into the water after your walking stick. The schoolmaster has become a little boy, who long ago took the cows to pasture. And you yourself are at the same time so small that you cannot tie your bootstraps yourself, but also so big and old that you have many small children that you must prepare sandwiches for. It goes quite naturally that a house becomes a cat, and a horse becomes a tree, and your book becomes a gingerbread. You think that's just how it should be. You would not be surprised if you suddenly became seventy miles tall and a thousand years old.

There are fantastic and beautiful pleasures on the Feather Isles. But not far from there are the Thistle Islands. Many arrive there, who have steered the wrong course in this world and are afflicted with laziness or a bad conscience. There is also a cave, which at the entrance resembles the Feather Isles' cave, and this causes many people to mistake the two. You will notice the differences soon enough. A slippery walk in the hard, rugged terrain leads to the cave of the Thistle Islands. The damp walls are covered with mould, and the ceilings are festooned with cobwebs. The rose beds of the Feather Isles have been transformed into nettles, the murmuring streams have been transformed into rapids and the chirping of birds into croaking crows. There is a high tower, from which one constantly seems to fall, and a deep bog, from which one fails to work one's way out. Strange and ugly figures move around on their heads. And in the dark night, a white angel with charcoal draws on the walls the evil deeds of the unfortunate, false, envious, and greedy wanderers.

No, we certainly do not want to travel to the Thistle Islands and to Lady Nightmare[1], who lives there. We would much prefer to travel to the Feather Isles because a good friend lives there. An old, old man sits at the entrance of the cave; yes, he is so old that when Adam first fell asleep under a tree in Paradise, the Sandman[2] was already standing by his side, spreading a blanket of roses over him. A long white beard flows down from the venerable old man's chin; around his waist he wears a red velvet belt. His long white coat, his blue socks and his yellow shoes are all woven from the softest down. When he extends his hand to you, that hand is as smooth as the finest cotton, and when he gently touches your eyelids, they become sweetly heavy. There is nothing so caressingly soft as his voice, when, like the slow rustling of leaves or the humming of bumblebees, he sings good little children to sleep, and his eyes are so gentle that the most frightened little girls like to sneak up and in his friendly embrace lean their curly heads against his bosom.

Oh, those beautiful eyes, if you knew how God's love and mercy shine in them, you would love him even more. For when the merciful God looked down on the first paradise, he sent a good angel to close the eyes of men in the dark night; and then when God saw so much toil and sorrow on earth, he sent the same good angel to give people rest and forgetfulness. And this good angel was the Sandman, death's older brother: therefore, a glimmer of the depths of eternity shines in his beautiful eyes. And all people know him, love him, and give him different names; but most of all he loves all children, for he cares for them most tenderly. When they are so small, so small that they do not know their own mother, then they already know him, and he sits by their cradle day and night, and when they grow larger, he takes them in his arms and brings the good children to the Feather Isles, and he really wants to bring even the wicked and disobedient youngsters there, but they themselves do not want to go. Then the Sandman worries that they must be doing so badly on the Thistle Islands, and he listens constantly to hear if they repent of their misadventures, so that he may gladly receive them again on the rose beds. Because he loves the children so much, he often plays tricks on them. It is he who, in the evening, sprinkles sand in their eyes and paints the roses of the Feather Isles on their cheeks. It is he who tricks the boys into lazily stretching at their school desks and the girls to yawn while practicing scales on the piano. Yes, he also usually comes uninvited to meetings of high lords and councillors, or to the speeches of learned professors and to students studying grammar, and soon all these men and women feel an inexplicable longing for a nap. Old women and men at church services are often severely affected by the Sandman. They nod and nod, and when the pastor preaches, it becomes a gentle sighing in their ears. The Sandman is being mischievous, but he is also testing them to see if they are serious about going to church. Those who have been to the Feather Isles know best how good he is. He understands perfectly how to give his guests the bedrooms that suit them well: the weary labourer in the half dark halls lit by starlight and the dance-tired girl in rose-coloured moonlit chambers. There, he sprinkles cherry blossoms over them and lets his sweetest dreamchildren flutter around them.

Do you know about dreamchildren? Oh, who does not know them? Yes, it depends. Do you know that they are the little boys and girls of the night, who are allowed by the Sandman to fly down from the stars in the vault of the evening sky, and it happens sometimes that they escape through the clouds even during the day. They are beautiful beings, woven of light and shadow; therefore, in an instant they can transform and take on any guise whatsoever. They dress in all possible and impossible shapes and imitate human life, just as the mirror imitates the human image. They carry you, in the blink of an eye, a thousand miles from here and bring you straight back again. They promise you everything you most enjoy, and you are so glad, so happy, but the next moment you have forgotten everything. They play shadow games for you, and you find yourself taking part; they play blind man's bluff with you, and you'll never catch them. Yes, they sometimes pretend to predict what will happen in the future, and if it happens, it will happen, but if it does not happen, it will not happen. Dreams flow like mysterious streams.

Only bad dreams live on the Thistle Islands. Wretched are those who fall for their nightmarish tricks. They let the dreamer fall into the lake, and he does not fall, but he thinks he is falling. They let him go on a dark road and meet a robber, or they tease him with an angry dog and a vicious bull. The robber does not hurt him, the dog does not bite him, the bull does not gore him, but that's what it looks like. It's just too crazy. Do not travel to the Thistle Islands!

Many inscriptions shine on the golden walls of the Feather Isles' cave, and he who has time to read them will certainly never suffer from a lack of beautiful fairy tales. It's a shame that you so seldom have time for that, because the many willing dreamchildren are always at hand to clean up the walls with their soft dust-brushes, and then the shining writing is swept away. I knew a little boy once; he was with the Sandman on the Feather Isles every night and understood the remarkable art of capturing dreams. He learned from a spider on the rose bush to tie nets of sunset glow and moonlight. He laid out the nets between sunset and sunrise and the dreamchildren were caught up in the nets. So, he caught the easy-going children of the night, and threw them into cages of poppy stalks. Then he had time to read the golden inscriptions, and after he read them, he released the dreamchildren from the poppy cage. The Sandman laughed and the next night sent one hundred and fifteen crazy dreamchildren to dance around the boy. But the boy had already read all the fairy tales and is happy to tell them to anyone who wants to hear. There are two of them in this book, namely 'Little Lasse' and 'Forest Bear', there are probably many others.

Forest Bear

Long ago in the city of Raumo, there was a rich merchant named Kovalyov[1]. He had a good head for business, and owned many ships which imported coffee, sugar, ginger, cardamom, and nutmeg from foreign countries. He always had good luck with his ships, except for the largest, named Neptune. This ship was commanded by Captain Forrest and brought cotton from America. Out on the ocean, the cotton caught fire and the burning Neptune sank with all its cargo. The captain drowned as well because he wanted to be the last to leave the ship.

Mr. Kovalyov mourned the precious ship in which he had invested so much of his hopes and capital. He could not forgive Captain Forrest for the cotton catching fire. Why would the captain buy such cotton? Maybe it did not catch fire by itself? Maybe sailors had gone into the hold with a naked light? Why hadn't Captain Forrest kept better order on board? And was it a coincidence that he was called Forrest when you hear about forest fires so often?

The ship's crew members were examined under oath upon returning home. Everyone swore that Captain Forrest had maintained the best discipline and had been the most skilled captain with whom they had ever sailed. But Kovalyov did not believe this. Captain Forrest had borrowed money from his boss and Kovalyov now sought repayment from the widow. The tragedy had made Captain Forrest's widow poor and she had a little boy named Björn to care for. She lost her small farm to Kovalyov's foreclosure and did not know how to support herself and her dear boy. However, she happened to be pretty, which can be a blessing but in this case was unfortunate. One day, Mr. Kovalyov, who was a widower, dressed up in a blue tailcoat with shiny buttons, red vest and white trousers, just like the Russian flag, and showed up at Mrs. Forrest's door and said to her:

"My dear lady, your husband has destroyed my ship; why did you associate with such a man? But I would like to forgive your imprudence. I want to do you the great honour of making you my wife and I hope that you will be very happy about it."

The poor widow was not happy at all but what could she do? She had a little boy who was cold and hungry, so she sadly said yes and quickly became Mrs. Kovalyov. Little Björn was included in the transaction and became Mr. Kovalyov's stepson. Kovalyov's own son, who now became Björn's stepbrother, was called Moisey. He was raised with sweet cakes and almond milk, wore tight velvet clothes, lived with his father, and did whatever he wanted. Björn had to eat hard bread with the servants, sleep on straw in their quarters, walk around in rough, worn-out clothes and serve as an errand boy. He was forced to work hard, was unjustifiably beaten, and was pushed around by Moisey. He was called by the nickname 'Forest Bear' instead of Björn[2] Forrest. That was supposed to sound so witty! One would hope for a better and happier upbringing, but it's not always bad to work hard. Moisey became a wastrel, lazy and incompetent, but Björn grew up big and strong, and became both humble and good at everything. Sometimes, when Moisey hit Björn and blamed him for his own stupidity, Björn wanted to run away as far as the road could take him. But then he realized his mother would weep, so he did not leave. She had hard days as well, but she took delight in her son. When Mr. Kovalyov was out on the ships and Moisey made himself sick eating figs, Mrs. Kovalyov called her little Björn to her, washed and combed his hair, gave him wheat bread with milk, taught him to read and admonished him to always be patient, diligent and loving, to always tell the truth, to fear God and trust in God's protection.

"Do not fret, my boy," said the mother, "They may mock you now as 'Forest Bear', but God will still make a proper man of you."

"Do you think so, Mamma?" asked Björn.

"Yes, I'm sure of it," said the mother.

"I will do my best," said Björn.

One summer, the rich Mr. Kovalyov sailed on his ship Apollo to Stockholm and took the two boys with him. They sailed across the Åland Sea with good winds and beautiful weather. Moisey lounged in his cabin and read novels. Björn was the cabin boy, running everyone's errands. He had sluiced the deck, washed the dishes, polished boots, been up to the crow's nest to clear the mainsail and climbed out on the bowsprit to sheet the jib, when Mr. Kovalyov said to him:

"Forest Bear!"

"Yes, Boss?" Björn replied. He never called his stepfather anything different.

"Clean my pipes!"

"Will do, Boss!"

"Be careful with the large, silver-plated meerschaum pipe. Remember, you rascal, she cost a hundred crowns."

"Sure thing, Boss!"

Björn was standing by the railing on the foredeck, cleaning the pipes, when Moisey stepped up behind him, pulled on his sweater and said:

"What are you doing, Forest Bear?"

"I'm cleaning the Boss's pipes."

"Come here, I'll help you!" said Moisey, grabbing the large

meerschaum pipe and knocking it against the railing, as he sometimes saw his father do. But the pipe bowl was loose on the shaft and without a lanyard. So, it fell into the Åland Sea with a splash.

Björn stood there flabbergasted, as if he himself had fallen into the sea. But Moisey was ingenious and said:

"Why did you shove me?"

"How have I shoved you?" Björn asked in surprise.

"Of course you have," Moisey said. And straightaway, as he saw his father approaching, Moisey pretended to be sobbing and shouted out:

"Why did you push me, so that Father's best pipe fell into the sea?"

Mr. Kovalyov was the kind of man who lost all reason when he became angry.

"I see," he said, "it is not enough for your father to burn down my best ship; now you throw my most expensive pipe into the sea! Boatswain, let down the ship's jolly boat[3], throw Forest Bear into that, and let him travel alone!"

The boatswain looked very taken aback, but did not dare say no. Within a few minutes, the jolly boat was lowered, Björn was put in it, and the boatswain barely had time to throw him a loaf of bread.

"Start rowing and find my pipe!" shouted Mr. Kovalyov from the afterdeck.

The ship Apollo was making good speed in the fresh wind, and soon the little jolly boat was left far behind. Björn was so astonished; he began to ask himself if he really had pushed his stepbrother. An honest boy cannot always comprehend how another boy could lie. The ship Apollo sailed even farther away from him, until it seemed like a small white dot far away on the horizon. Björn noticed to his horror that he was now all alone in a small boat out on the open sea. Large fish splashed around him, dolphins sprayed jets of water, seals gazed with their dark doglike heads up over the waves. None of them could help him. The wind picked up and the sea seemed to be dressed in white foam. Evening fell, it became dark, and Forest Bear drifted in his boat towards night and death.

Well, who in the whole wide world would care about an abandoned wretch like little Forest Bear? No one would ask about him; he would sink into the sea and the waves would crash over his head. The next morning not even a bubble would mark his watery demise. The ships would sail on the blue sea over him, and the sailors would sing their merry shanties, just as before.

Someone would still miss him - his mother. When Björn thought of her, he began to weep. But after he cried for a while, he became hungry and began to nibble at the hard bread. This strengthened him and cheered him up. God sometimes appears to have some solace to comfort the forsaken. Björn did not know how it came about but suddenly his mood became optimistic. He remembered his mother's admonition to trust in God when in great distress and danger.

'Should I try to pray?' he thought to himself.

Prayer was not an immediate success. The waves became high, the jolly boat swung around like a leaf, was lifted high up and sank down again as if in a deep valley. It was not easy to keep his thoughts together. Björn recited from memory all the prayers his mother had taught him; they were rote, words without meaning, but soon he began to create his own prayers.

"Dear God," he said, "I am a poor little boy, my hand is weak, and I can do nothing against the mighty sea. But you, God, are great and strong. You are much more powerful than the waves of the sea. The storm obeys your commands and if you forbid them, night and death can do me no harm. I trust in you, my God. You've always been good to me, and you would certainly never abandon me. So, preserve me now on the dark sea; let thy angels go forth upon the great waters, and command the waves not to hurt me. I want to be your child, my God, and sleep in your arms. Thank you, thank you! Good night, dear God! Good night, dark seas, and bright stars in the sky! Good night, Mamma!"

And the little Forest Bear fell sound asleep on the bottom of the jolly boat in the middle of the open sea.

It was dark now, and one could hardly see that, far away on the horizon, a soft and light-green shore rose above the foaming waves. It was the Feather Isles. The Sandman[4] sat there on the velvety grass. He looked out over the desolate seascape and noticed the little jolly boat, in which Forest Bear drifted like the wind's plaything. The Sandman cast out his lines, as fine as spider silk, drew the jolly boat to the Feather Isles and lay Björn down among the rose-petal beds in his domain's gleaming silver hall. Here, a thousand dreamchildren in variegated butterfly costumes were immediately at hand; they fluttered lightly over the waters and brought Björn's beloved mother to him. He felt her soft hand on his head, he felt her kiss on his forehead, he heard her dear voice, which whispered in his ear:

"Be in good spirits, my boy; be always truthful, patient and humble; God will protect you. Forest Bear will still become a proper man."

The Sandman stood quietly and motionless by the boy's side. Only one of the dreamchildren buzzed for a long time like a bee around the boy's ears and shouted insistently:

"Three things! Three things!"

"Be quiet," said Björn to the dreamchild; "What would I do with your 'Three things'? Dreams are like babbling streams."

The night passed; the morning brightened. Björn thought that the roof rose above him and became a clear sky, the walls widened and became translucent air, the floor began to sway and became a gentle sea swell. All the diamonds and crystals in the Feather Isle's cave faded, a delicate, pink veil fell over everything, and the slow music, which hummed throughout the cave all night, dissolved into the monotonous murmur of the sea's waves.

Björn felt a chill around his head, opened his eyes and looked around in amazement. Above him stretched the sky, below him was the blue sea and around him the cool morning air. Björn lay on the bottom of his jolly boat, and his hat had blown from his head into the sea. 'I have been dreaming,' he thought, 'and God has protected me. Thank you, dear God!'

Then he sat up to eat from the loaf of bread he still had left. He felt thirsty; the sea water was salty and did not taste good, but the Baltic Sea is not so salty that its water cannot be drunk in an emergency.

To his great astonishment, Björn saw, awfully close to him, a big ship without a mast, drifting helplessly. It had been a stormy night and the waves were still high, but the worst of the storm was over. Björn took hold of his oars and rowed towards the ship.

Yes, it was a large, heavily laden ship, which had sprung a leak during the storm. The masts had been cut down, so that it would not capsize. It barely floated anymore, it was filled with water and had been abandoned by its crew. Alongside the ship, Björn shouted "Ahoy, there". Nobody answered. Then he boldly climbed up onto the ship's deck.

Here, rigging, goods, tools and debris were strewn about in great disarray. The cargo hold contained much valuable merchandise, but there seemed to be no living creature aboard. Björn became ill at ease and wanted to get back into his boat when a pitiful bleating from the bow reached his ears.

It was a goat, tied to a cleat. Björn undid the goat's rope, grabbed a loaf of bread floating on the water and was ready to climb back down into the jolly boat. But as he waded in the water past the steps down to the ship's cabin, he saw many things floating around, and at once he remembered the stubborn dream. 'I may as well go for three things, as I already have two!' thought Björn, grabbing a small mahogany box which floated by the stairs, and then he hurried with the goat, the bread, and the box down into his jolly boat. He was just in time. He had not rowed many fathoms from the ship before he heard a strange noise - the large ship sank in a great whirlpool of water, and soon the waves covered the tragedy of a defective hull.

For two days and two nights, Björn drifted on the sea in the jolly boat. He shared his bread with the goat, and the goat gave him her milk. On the morning of the third day a ship appeared. It came closer, having noticed the boy's sweater tied to an oar like an emergency flag. The crew took him on board, and he sailed with them to Stockholm.

"Well, little lad, to whom in this city shall I now take you?" asked the captain.

"I do not know anyone in Stockholm," Björn replied. "Let me stay on board as a cabin boy and learn the job. I want to become a capable sailor, like my father."

"Well," replied the captain. "Maybe that could work out. My last cabin boy has left me - he had been pining for his mother's baking. Stay here and I will sell your goat, and for the money you can buy yourself better clothes. Your former boss must not have been very generous towards you."

"He gave me food," replied the boy.

"Yes, and also called you Forest Bear; the disrespect is noticeable from your clothes," said the captain. "But now Forest Bear will become a proper man."

That resonated with Björn. He had now heard this same phrase for the third time.

The next day, Björn went out into Stockholm to buy new clothes. At a street corner, a crowd of people stood and read a placard posted there. Björn stopped and asked what was going on.

"Oh," said a broad-shouldered foundry worker with his hands in his trouser pockets, "all the young rascals must now be curious! It does not concern you. A fine gentleman promises a thousand riksdaler[5] as a reward to anyone who can reclaim a small casket from the Åland Sea. Better if you go home and read your catechism!"

Björn remembered the small mahogany box which he had salvaged from the sinking ship. 'Three things!' the dreamchild had cried out to him.

In a hurry, Björn went back onboard his ship. The small casket had been left among the rubbish and old boots under a bed in the forecastle. Like an arrow, Björn went out into the city again with the casket under his ragged sweater and made his way to the noble gentleman's residence. There he was greeted at the gate by half a dozen servants with contemptuous looks.

"Be on your way, ragamuffin!" shouted the servants. "We have no coins for beggars."

"We'll see about that," Björn replied and pointed to his casket.

"What is that?" said the servants, reaching for the box. "Give us the casket, and you'll get paid tomorrow."

"No, I'm not that stupid," Björn said and held on to his casket.

But the tallest and strongest servant grabbed him by the collar and said:

"Thieving boy, confess that you stole the casket!"

"You're lying about that, no matter how tall you are," Björn answered and resisted with all his might. There was uproar and commotion until a gentleman in a grand dressing-gown opened the door and asked what was going on.

"Your Grace,' cried the servants, "here is a boy who stole a casket."

"I have never stolen," Björn shouted.

"Come in with your box, boy!" commanded the stern gentleman.

Björn entered bravely; he had a clear conscience.

The noble gentleman had scarcely caught sight of the casket before he snatched it from the boy's hands.

"My casket! My treasure!" he exclaimed, pressing a secret spring, and the lid sprang open. The least Björn expected to see were real pearls, but there were only a few yellowed sheets of paper in the box. 'There must have been something of value to promise so much money for!' thought Björn.

But the aristocratic gentleman said to him:

"My dear boy, you have rescued my honour and my fortune. I am accused of having embezzled the Crown's money, and these papers will prove my innocence. Tell me how you found the casket!"

Björn told of his adventure but kept quiet about how badly his stepfather had treated him.

"Looking at you, I see that you are an honest lad, "said the gentleman in his dressing-gown. "If you wish, I will deposit a thousand riksdaler on your behalf in the bank and give you written confirmation."

Yes, Björn was greatly pleased with that but what would he do with such great wealth? He thanked the noble gentleman, returned to his captain, and told him of his new fortune. The captain smiled and said:

"Well, Forest Bear, now that you are rich, you do not have to make a hard living at sea. You can be lazy and live off cakes for several years."

"No thank you, I'm not that daft," Björn replied. "Now I want to work properly and learn the sea-faring trade. So, in a few years I can become a boatswain and then a first mate ..."

"And then Captain?"

"Oh yes, and then Captain," Björn answered. He blushed at his extravagant ambition. "I want to use the money to learn navigation," he said, "and when I get my own ship, I want to sail to Raumo to fetch my mother ..."

"That's right, Forest Bear!' said the captain. "Hold that course, and God will help you."

Björn persevered like a grown man. For two years he was a cabin boy, grew stronger and stronger, began to walk wide legged, as sailors do, and then became a deckhand, then an able seaman, then a boatswain, then a first mate. He sailed around the world and endured hardship but was always hearty and happy. Over two winters he studied navigation, mathematics, and geography. He graduated with honours, became captain, and got his own ship to command. He was upright, skilful, and trustworthy; he did well. In a few years he took charge of his own beautiful ship, named 'She-Bear'.

One beautiful day there was great excitement in Raumo. An unfamiliar ship sailed in, the likes of which had never been seen. All the masts and blocks were fitted with brass, so that they shone in the sun like gold. The stern was gilded, in the bow a she-bear gleamed with silver, and 'She-Bear' was written on all the flags.

The whole town was intrigued. Everyone wanted to go down to the harbour to see the proud She-Bear, and not the least curious was old Mr. Kovalyov with his son Moisey. It had been bad for the businessman in recent years and now he had only his avarice and his old Apollo left. Moisey mostly lay on a sofa reading old newspapers. But now Moisey also wanted to go out to the harbour. Father and son rowed themselves out to She-Bear. There they humbly asked for the great honour of visiting the stately ship.

"Please climb aboard!" replied Captain Björn Forrest, who disguised his voice and did not let on that he knew his wicked stepfather and his vindictive son quite well. They would never have imagined that the young and handsome captain was their own former Forest Bear. They believed him to be a wealthy Englishman, taking a cruise to visit foreign lands.

The captain let them observe all the ship's marvels and then invited them to a nice dinner on board. He was a plain and frugal man, but now he brought forth delicacies and fine wines from all over the world. His guests could not help but marvel at the splendour of the ship and the delicious dinner; they were ready to burst with envy, and this amused Captain Björn.

When the guests, with many sweet yet sour words on their lips, wanted to give thanks and say goodbye, the captain asked, as if by chance, if Mrs. Kovalyov was still alive.

"Yes, she lives, poor woman," replied Kovalyov, "but she never goes out. She mourns her stupid, unfortunate son."

"Oh," said Björn. "Did she have a son?"

"Yes, of course. A very mean and stupid boy, who drowned in the Åland Sea fifteen years ago."

"Is it so certain that he drowned?" Björn asked.

"Unfortunately," Kovalyov sighed. "A heavy sea took him away, and he sank like a rock to the bottom."

"Why did he push me?" muttered Moisey.

"I have heard it said that he was unfairly accused and abandoned in a jolly boat on the open sea," Captain Björn recalled.

Moisey became red in the face and shouted: "Yes, but he was given a loaf of bread!"

"Will you be silent?" shouted Mr. Kovalyov.

Captain Björn looked them straight in the eye and now said in his natural voice: "I have heard it said that the boy is alive and wants to hold his stepfather to account. The entire crew can testify that the boy was abandoned on the high seas."

Now Kovalyov and Moisey's faces turned as pale as they had formerly been red. They couldn't help but deny everything.

"Oh really?" said Captain Björn. "I have read about another little boy back in ancient times; his name was Moses, not unlike Moisey. He was abandoned in a small basket on the River Nile but survived and become a great man. Do you not know that the waves obey God's will? It does not help to lie to God. What have you done to the little Forest Bear?"

Uh-oh - now it was all over for Mr. Kovalyov and his son Moisey. They recognized Forest Bear again, their consciences struck them, and they fell shakily to their knees, pleading that he might forgive them, they would never do such a thing again.

Forest Bear, who had now become the stern captain Björn Forrest, let them bleat on for a while, but then he said with tears in his eyes:

"Stand up, stepfather! Get up, Moisey! I did not come to redeem God's goodness toward me by being hard-hearted. No, I do not want to accuse you, it's all forgiven. Just give me back my mother, and we'll be good friends again!"

Behold, these words were like hail and sunshine at the same time! Mr. Kovalyov felt a stone fall from his heart, and his complexion turned dark red again. Moisey pretended to cry and eagerly fibbed that he never liked anyone in the world as much as he liked Forest Bear. Everyone made their way to the poor forsaken Mrs. Kovalyov, and no one can describe her feelings of amazement and happiness when she saw her son again. For fifteen years she had mourned the death of her little dear Forest Bear, and now he stood there, a tall and dashing sailor, very much alive. Now he had become a grown and successful man, just as she had predicted when he was little.

Forest Björn knew he would only become a happy man when he was reunited with his mother. Forthwith, he bought a beautiful farm for them both, they moved there and lived happily together for a whole year, while She-Bear lay at anchor in the harbour. But eventually, another beautiful 'she-bear' came into the house. Captain Björn became enamoured with a poor, hard-working Raumo girl, who could weave the finest lace, and she became his wife. After he had lived so happily for a while, he felt like going to sea again, now that his mother was no longer alone. As he enjoyed himself better at home, he did not sail now to the end of the earth; he travelled out every spring in May and returned in November with beautiful Christmas presents for those ashore: his mother, his 'she-bear' and his little 'bear cubs'. It was much better to dance with them around the cheerful Christmas tree than it had been to sit alone in a little jolly boat on the open sea.

Now, for Björn, everything was as it should be. But Mr. Kovalyov and his son Moisey would have preferred that the Forest Bear still sat in his jolly boat and had never come back. They were jealous of his good fortune, and they pondered night and day how they could become as rich as Forest Bear. He had told them of his adventures with the Sandman, the wrecked ship and the mahogany casket; he had jokingly mentioned the dreamchild, who shouted at him: - 'three things! three things'! Mr. Kovalyov and Moisey now put all this together and became more and more certain that there must have been magic involved. They convinced themselves that they could get rich the same way.

Yes, it could be done! The old Apollo, neglected and leaking, was still at anchor in the harbour. Kovalyov had it rigged anew, loaded it with tar and furs and sailed with his son to Stockholm, hoping that during the trip they would find a mahogany casket on the Åland Sea.

Everything had to be done as it had been when Forest Bear was abandoned on the open sea. Mr. Kovalyov threw a broken meerschaum pipe into the sea, pretended to be very angry with Moisey and cast him out in the ship's pinnace[3] onto the calm sea. In the pinnace was a bed with a feather mattress, a duvet, silk sheets and three pillows. Moisey was provided with four large bread buns, a tub of butter, a veal roast, two cheeses, a stack of pancakes, a jar of jam, a case of beer and six bottles of wine. Moisey himself was dressed in a wolfskin coat and high boots, and reclined on the soft cushions, smoking a cigar.

The tall ship sailed away, the pinnace was left alone, everything was calm. Moisey enjoyed a grand supper, drank beer, drank wine, smoked more cigars, and found the adventure quite satisfying. When it grew dark, he pulled the covers over his ears and fell sound asleep. He thought it completely unnecessary to say an evening prayer. During the night, a storm arose. Moisey slept while the storm drove the pinnace to the shores of the Thistle Islands. There Lady Nightmare sat on the rough rocks, looking for prey. She noticed Moisey, dragged him and the pinnace ashore, led him to a musty cave and laid him on a bed of nettles. That stung; it burned all over his body and lead lay on his eyelids and on his heart. The enchantress squeezed and pinched him black and blue, pulled his hair and laughed so much with mirth that the goatskin coat on her back burst. After running riot for a while, she threw Moisey back into the pinnace, pushed it off the beach, and let him go.

Moisey woke up lying in bilgewater, while the pinnace was thrown about like a ball by the waves. Terrified, he got up, but was knocked down again. His head ached; his body had been whipped with nettles. For three days he drifted around on the sea, could not move, could not eat, and was burnt by the sun. The adventure had become unpleasant. But on the third day the storm calmed down, and now Moisey wanted to have a good meal. Alas, the bread buns and cheeses had been soaked by seawater, the butter tub had fallen into the sea and the pancakes had become fish-food. Fortunately, there was still veal roast, beer and wine. Moisey ate and felt more at ease. His good mood continued as he saw a wrecked ship, without a mast, upon a stone reef. Moisey rowed to it: no one was on board; everything was in disarray and pieces of the cargo floated around in the ship. Moisey would have been able to salvage many items, but he only sought 'three things': a goat, a loaf of bread and a mahogany box. He did not find any goat, only a grey cat, nor any bread, but rather a tar bucket. If only he could now discover a casket. What luck! He found a round box, made not of mahogany but of aspen. With these precious three things, he rowed away contentedly from the wrecked ship.

It was evening: Moisey ate the veal roast, drank beer, fell asleep and drifted on the sea. When morning came Moisey woke up, felt hungry again and wanted to eat, but now the cat had eaten the rest of the roast veal. Even though she scratched him in the face, he was happy not to throw her into the sea; no, 'three things'; she must be allowed to live.

On the sixth day at sea, he had nothing left but wine - poor thing! He drank, he became giddy and lightheaded, and he would have fallen into the sea, when just then a cargo boat bearing wood from Åland happened to sail past.

"Catch hold of that boat and throw the drunkard in the scuppers!" cried the skipper to his only sailor. The sailor obeyed; Moisey was picked up. "Refresh him a little with the cat-o'-nine-tails, then he will be cheerful again!" said the skipper.

Moisey was refreshed and he paid to be taken to Raumo. When he got back to his father, he beat his fist on the table and asked why he had been left on the sea for six days.

"Alas, my dear boy," replied Mr. Kovalyov, "if you only knew what had happened! That night, after you were set off in the pinnace, a terrible storm arose. We cut down the masts, but the ship drifted onto a reef, and no one had time to think about you. Alas, my beautiful Apollo! My tar barrels and my precious furs! They were more valuable than a bucket filled with silver and gold. Alas! Woe!" And Mr. Kovalyov wept bitterly, for nothing was more heartfelt to him than when he lost money.

"But what about you?" he continued sobbing. "Did you find your casket?"

"Yes, look here!" said Moisey. "Nothing ventured, nothing gained. I have been pummelled, scratched, pinched, bitten, squeezed, poked, and whipped, so that I am quite put out of joint. But that doesn't matter. I have slept in seawater, been burnt by the sun, robbed, got drunk on wine and taken the lash, but that doesn't matter either. These things came to pass. Now I am so rich that Forest Bear is only a mole compared to me."

"Dear boy, are we really that rich now?" exclaimed the father.

"I say I'm rich, but that has nothing to do with you, father," Moisey countered harshly.

"But my dearest boy, I'm poor now. Shouldn't we share, like good friends?"

"Not so much as a farthing," Moisey replied.

"Alas, Moisey, can you be so ungrateful to your gracious father! Where do you have your casket?"

"Here!" exclaimed Moisey proudly, showing the box.

"What on earth?" shouted Mr. Kovalyov. "Is that the box? But then you have been on board our own Apollo!"

"I have been on board the Apollo?" asked Moisey.

"Yes, that's where you have been. Great treasures, pah! What do you think the box contains?"

Moisey explained that Forest Bear had not opened the casket until he got to Stockholm, and so Moisey had not dared to open the box until he was back in Raumo. What would it contain, likely gold dust and diamonds?

"Gold dust? Alas, you unlucky duck! Open it yourself and see!"

Moisey opened the box with a trembling hand. What did he find in there? He found his father's old wig, which was to be refurbished in Stockholm.

Mr. Kovalyov, in all his sorrow, could not refrain from laughing. This angered Moisey, who thought he had already taken enough aggravation.

"Now listen, Father!" he said. "Wasn't Apollo loaded with tar and fur?"

"Unfortunately, yes," sighed father. "And now everything is at the bottom of the sea."

"But I have salvaged something."

"Is that possible? What have you recovered?"

"This tar bucket!"

"Oh, for shame! Have you not salvaged any of my precious furs?"

"Of course I have," Moisey said.

"Was it one of the grey ones?"

"Yes, it was one of the grey ones."

"Well, that is some consolation. My dear boy, where do you have the fur?"

"It is running in here on its own four feet," Moisey replied. And the ship's cat arched its back towards its surprised master.

"Oh, you great lutefisk[6]!" Mr. Kovalyov shouted angrily, took his walking stick and let it dance vigorously on Moisey's back. And the cane danced, and the cat hissed, and Moisey Kovalyov imagined himself to be back on the Thistle Islands. But Forest Bear did not hear them: he sat far away teaching his 'bear cubs' to climb upon his back as if on the rigging of a large ship.

Knut Spelevink

Knut was a poor boy without a father or mother and lived in a small cottage with his grandmother on the shores of Pärlebank. He had a shirt, a sweater, a pair of trousers and a hat; in the summer he didn't need more. In the winter, he had woollen stockings and birch bark shoes; that wasn't so bad. He was cheerful and always happy, but also always hungry. It is an uncommon skill to be able to be hungry and cheerful at the same time.

Another hardship was that his kind grandmother seldom had enough food so that the boy could eat his fill. She spun wool and sent Knut to sell the yarn at Mr. Peterman's large manor house, called Åsa, a few miles away. When Knut returned with the money paid for the yarn, the old woman bought flour to bake bread-rolls. Grandmother also had a fyke net (a fish trap), so sometimes there would be fish to eat when fisherman Jonas' sons helped Knut to lay out the fyke net. If there was a good money coming in for the yarn, sour milk would be a treat, and some potatoes could be grown in a little vegetable patch by the cottage. But they were not often so well off, and though Knut's little stomach often grumbled for more, he always remained cheerful.

One morning he sat hungry on the shores of Pärlebank, picking up yellow stones, which looked like soft, warm, boiled potatoes. Poor Knut, they were not fit for eating; laughing, he threw them away. Then he noticed something between the stones. Knut picked it up and saw it was a small pipe made from a reed, which children at the shore often enjoy carving. It was nothing fancy at all, but Knut wanted to see if the pipe made any noise. Yes, it did make a sound, he could play three notes on it: 'pu', 'py' and 'pi'. Knut stuffed the pipe into his shirt pocket.

It happened to be a day of fasting: Knut had not even had breakfast. 'If only I now were sitting in Mr. Peterman's kitchen at Åsa!' he thought to himself, imagining that he could smell fried sprats.

He had to do something. He sat down on a rock by the shore and started fishing. But the fish weren't biting. The sea was as smooth as glass after a storm the day before, the sun was shining, the swell rolled lazily towards the beach and kissed Undine Marina's footprints[1] in the sand.

'I wonder what Grandma has for lunch today,' Knut thought to himself.

Then a wave came up so high that it washed over Knut's bare feet, and there was a murmur in the swell:

"Knut, have you discovered the princess' magic pipe? One can blow three notes on the pipe: 'pu' to sleep, 'py' to weep and 'pi' to laugh."

"How about that!" said Knut. "Is it a magic pipe? On your way, wave; I have found the pipe and intend to keep it."

The wave mumbled something indiscernible, rolled out again and did not come back. Knut took the pipe out of his pocket and looked at it.

"So, you can do magic, can you? Well, conjure me up a fish on the hook!" And at once he blew 'pu', 'pu'.

Not long after he had blown, first a bleak, then a roach, and finally a pike floated to the surface of the water, lying on their sides as if they were sleeping.

'Fresh fish are common here!' Knut thought and continued to blow. After a while, the entire surface of the water by the shore was covered with floating fish: minnows, roach, vendace, perch, bream, ide, pikeperch, whitefish, salmon and all the quick-tailed fry that live in the sea.

'This will be a grand fish harvest!' Knut reckoned and ran up to the cottage to get a landing net. When he returned, he saw the beach filled with waterfowl. The seagulls were the most greedy and ungenerous; their cries of "Krak, krak" could be heard miles away. But many others came to the party: mallards, mergansers, goldeneyes, wild geese, even swans. All these predatory guests were hard at work devouring the floating fish, and amid the swarm a large osprey swooped down, seizing in its claws a nine-pound salmon.

"Hold up, you thieves!" said Knut, picking up rocks from the beach, and began to throw them at the birds. Some stones hit wings, others hit legs, but no one seemed inclined to let go of their prey. Then a shot rang out, then one or two more from the nearby strait. Some of the birds now lay on their side and floated on the water, just like the fish. The shots continued to crack out, until the whole swarm of birds was either shot down, or otherwise scattered screaming in all directions.

A boat with three hunters approached the beach to collect their prey. It was Mr. Peterman, who had rowed out with two of his friends to hunt birds. They landed ashore in good spirits.

"Look at you, Knut!" said Mr. Peterman. "How could you have gathered so many birds here at Pärlebank?"

"I played for the fishes, and the birds wanted to keep them company," Knut answered smartly.

"My, you've become a skilled musician," said Mr. Peterman. "From now on, your name will be Knut Spelevink[2]."

"Okay with me," said Knut. - He did not have a surname until now and he could just as easily be called Spelevink as Andersson, Söderlund, or Mattsson.

"But listen, Knut Spelevink, why do you look so down-hearted today? You're skinny as a beanpole," said Mr. Peterman.

"Why wouldn't I feel bad, having seen so much food and not having eaten anything since yesterday's lunch?" Knut answered in his cheerful way.

"I see, I see. Come to Åsa for dinner today, since you have provided us with such a good catch! But don't come until four o'clock, so there is time for the birds to be plucked and roasted."

"I thank you most humbly," Knut replied. He thought to himself: 'That is rather late for someone who has not eaten since yesterday's lunch.'

Mr. Peterman rowed away; Knut went back to Grandma.

"Well, Knut, have you caught any fish today?"

"I've seen plenty, but the birds ate up the fish and Mr. Peterman shot the birds."

"That was unfortunate, Knut. We have nothing else for dinner but two herrings, four potatoes and half a loaf of bread."

"Don't worry, Grandma! You should eat; I'm invited to Åsa for dinner. I'll put a piece of cheese in my pocket and bring it back for you."

"Do not take the shortcut through Kiikkala forest, Knut; not only do the elves live there but also three troll kings: the mountain king, the snow king and the forest king. Better to go along the shoreline where it is safer, though beware of the mermaid!"

"The shoreline route is so long, Grandma, and I have not eaten anything since yesterday's lunch."

"Well, go where you want, but do not think about food, it will lead to temptation."

"No, Grandma, I will think about my next catechism (bible-studies) test[3]."

Knut went along the shore, thinking about his catechism, but when he came to the shortcut, he thought: 'Surely, being so hungry, I would be a fool to walk two miles instead of one.'

So, he took the shortcut through Kiikkala forest, testing himself on the catechism while walking through the woods. He had not gone far before he saw a small, scrawny, old man, dragging a cart loaded with twelve iron bars.

"Good day, Knut Spelevink," said the old man. "Why do you look so unwell today?"

"Why wouldn't I look poorly, not having had anything to digest but catechism since yesterday's lunch? But how do you know my new name?"

"I know everyone's names," said the old man.

"May I help you? That load has you all out of breath."

"Haul away, if you want, Spelevink."

Knut pushed the cart along, and soon they came to a large rocky outcrop in the woods.

"This is where I live," said the old man. "Come in, so I can reward you for helping me with that cargo."

As the old man went through an entrance below the outcrop, Knut's stomach said: 'Follow!' and Knut followed. Soon they were in a large underground palace, where everything shone with gold, silver and precious stones.

"Do you live here?" asked Knut.

"Of course," said the old man. "I am the mountain king, and tomorrow I will celebrate my daughter's wedding. All my people are so busy that I have to get my food myself from the forge."

"Was that iron that you dragged along in the cart?" asked Knut.

"Iron bars, my boy, iron bars of the best kind. A much superior grade than simple pig iron. These iron bars are my favourite dish, especially when white-hot. Have you ever eaten iron bars?"

"No," said Knut; "not that I can remember."

"Then you shall get to taste something extra nice. See here, I will put two bars into the hot oven. In three minutes, they will glow white; crawl then into the oven and slice them up while they're hot!"

"Thank you so much, but I'd rather you give me a bread-roll with butter and a nice bowl of yoghurt."

"Look, you don't understand how good this is! Clamber quickly into the oven, the iron is already red."

"I can't. It's far too hot."

"What kind of talk is that? "It's just a comfortable heat," the old man growled and would have tried with all his might to push Knut into the burning oven. But the one who got to his feet first was Knut. He ran for dear life, managed to find the way out and was soon back on the forest road.

"Grandma was right," thought Knut. "I should concentrate on my catechism test."

While Knut was thinking about the difficult questions, he began to wonder, 'Why do I feel so cold?' The reason soon became clear - there was a big mountain of snow in the middle of summer. 'That is strange,' Knut thought. 'But where can I get some hot food?'

With these words, thinking about food, he stepped into the snow, but all at once he plummeted into a deep hole and found himself in a magnificent palace of glistening ice. It was bright with starlight and moonlight, all the halls were adorned with mirrors of shiny ice, all the floors strewn with diamonds of hoarfrost. Clumsy snowmen tumbled about on their stomachs across the floors. Only one stood up straight; it was a long, stiff giant, icicles in his hair, icicles in his beard, a nightgown of paper-thin ice and shoes of frozen berry juice.

"Well, good day to you, Knut Spelevink," said the giant: "Why do you look so out of sorts today?"

"Why wouldn't I look below par, not having been given anything but a hot bar of iron since yesterday's lunch?" replied Knut with chattering teeth.

"You're too hot, young man, you're too hot," said the giant. "I'm the snow king, I'm rearing all my subjects to be blocks of ice, and I will make you become a block of ice as well. Chief snowman, dip the boy seven times in ice-cold water, hang him on a peg, and let him freeze!"

"No, wait a minute," Knut said. "Rather give me a mug of hot posset, I'm already an ice cube!"

"Snowman, give him a piece of frozen mercury and a mug of shivers before dipping him!" commanded the giant.

Knut would have risen to his feet, but it was already too late. The chief snowman grabbed him by the collar; it would have been the end of him if he had not happened to get hold of his pipe. What else could Knut do but to blow the pipe, and this time it sounded 'pi', 'pi'.

Quickly the tall snow king's features twisted into a grin, which might have signalled mirth, but was really anger over his need to laugh, which unexpectedly gained power over him. He laughed, in fact he laughed so much that the icicles fell from his hair and chin, his back became crooked, and finally his head fell off and broke into pieces. All the snowmen fell apart with laughter, the chief snowman tumbled over and became slush, the ice walls crashed down into small shards and the whole snow mountain turned into a dizzying snowstorm. Only with the greatest effort could Knut keep his lips together and blow, he laughed so much. In the middle of the blizzard, he found himself back again on the forest road, the snowmelt ran away in torrents, and it was full summer again.

'Now I must be more careful,' Knut thought, striding steadily forward while trying to remember the answers to his pastor's biblical questions: 'What is that'[3]. But he had not gone far before he came across the most beautiful green forest hillside where red wild-strawberries glistened amongst the grass. 'It can't be dangerous to gather just a few strawberries, especially since I won't get fed until late afternoon,' thought Knut and stepped up onto the forest slope. No sooner was he there before he realized that what he considered strawberries were really many thousands of lovely little elves in red skirts. They were no taller than strawberry stalks and danced merrily around a green tussock on which sat their queen, who was three inches tall.

"Good day to you, Knut Spelevink," said the elf-queen. "Why do you look so glum today?"

"Why wouldn't I look fed up? I've been offered nothing since yesterday's lunch other than a hot bar of iron and some frozen mercury? I thought you were a strawberry."

"The poor lad, he is famished," said the elf-queen to her maid. "Give him a drop of dew and a mosquito leg, so that he can properly satisfy his hunger!'

"Thank you very much," Knut replied. "But maybe I could just get a tub of strawberries and a pail of milk?"

"What a gross ruffian!" said the elf-queen, greatly offended by such an excessive appetite. "Do you know, man-child, that you came into my kingdom without a passport and trampled to death thirty-three of my loyal subjects, so that there is only a red stain where they once stood? Forest spiders, do your duty!"

No sooner was this said, than a legion of long-legged spiders climbed down from the trees and began to bind Knut up with countless fine cobwebs. Knut did not like such a cruel joke; he pushed aside the cobwebs and wished to get back to the forest road but could not move from the spot. His feet were entangled in ever stronger nets, his arms were stuck to his shirt, his eyes were glued shut, and he finally fell over in the grass.

He could not see anything, but he heard the whole forest hillside laughing. The elves made a ring and danced around and over him, pinched his cheeks like mosquitoes, and were overjoyed at such a hilarious prank.

"Now lie here and starve, until you will be satisfied by a drop of dew and a mosquito leg!" they said.

Knut made a plea. "Listen, little elves," he said, "I'd be happy to eat a small piece of reed, which I carry in my shirt pocket. Would anyone be so good as to stick it in my mouth?"

To see such a greedy man-child eating a reed greatly amused the elves. Four of them climbed into his shirt pocket and together pulled out the magic pipe, which they managed with great difficulty to stick into his mouth. Then they began to dance even more merrily around and over him, so that the forest hillside resounded with their laughter, sounding like a swarm of mosquitoes.

Knut quickly began to blow, and this time it sounded 'py', 'py'. At once the cheerful laughter ended on the forest slopes, and soon a hundred thousand sobs were heard all around, not unlike the sound one hears in the summer when a cloudburst falls in a deluge on the hillside. Knut could not see, but he gathered that the elves were weeping, and thought it poignant that such droll creatures could sob so mournfully.

"Release me, and you will laugh again," Knut said to the elves.

To laugh is the elves' greatest pleasure, and they laugh away their short lives in the long summer evenings. At once hundreds chased away the spiders, released the prisoner's arms and legs, and opened his glued-up eyes. Knut could now see his little tormentors and was mean enough to blow another 'py'. Oh, how the poor little creatures grimaced and lamented! They really wanted to laugh, yet they still had to cry because of the dreadful 'py' sound! Knut did not have the heart to torment them any longer. His whistling shifted to the 'pi', 'pi' tone, and then the fairies went mad with joy. They took such high jumps, colliding with the larks in the sky above, that some of those birds fell straight down on Knut, who had to shake them off. He did not notice that one of the elves had fallen into his shirt pocket and did not come out again.

"Goodbye, little elves!" said Knut and briskly continued his walk on the forest road. 'I must beware of the forest king,' thought Knut; 'he could be the worst. Now, the answers to my pastor's catechism test: 'What is that ...'?'

After a while, Knut came to a cloudberry bog by the side of the road. 'It can't be so bad to grab a few cloudberries here in passing, since I won't get any food until four o'clock this afternoon,' Knut thought. There was a large, fallen spruce, and to get to the bog, Knut had to step over the spruce. Barely was he in the middle of its dense, leafy branches, before the spruce, to Knut's great dismay, stood up and roared in a gruff voice:

"Good day to you, Knut Spelevink, you look so morose today."

Knut was hanging high above the ground in the top of the spruce, but took courage and answered: "Why wouldn't I look miserable, not having been offered any food since yesterday's lunch, other than a hot iron bar, frozen mercury, a drop of dew and a mosquito leg?"

"Well, why are you disturbing my afternoon nap?" asked the tree. "Don't you know that I am the forest king and rule over all trees and bogs within seventy kilometres? Here you see my castle; don't I live well?"

Knut, who saw nothing but wild wasteland, dared to ask most humbly if he could be allowed to descend and pick some cloudberries.

"What nonsense! Cloudberries?" roared forest king. "Take the pine ladle and scoop up seven helpings of moss; I call it real food, it's my favourite dish."

"Maybe I could get a load of applesauce and a reasonably large pot filled with wild honey?" inquired Knut.

"Applesauce? I will make applesauce of you for disturbing my afternoon nap. Golden eagle, I give you the boy, you can hack him into stewing-steak for your chicks!"

Now Knut noticed a huge eagle, which sat at the top of the tree and looked down at him with predatory eyes. He could not jump down; the spruce branches held his arms and legs; he would soon be torn limb from limb. Knut Spelevink had never eaten a meat stew, but no matter how much he liked food, he found it disagreeable to become food for an eagle.

In this precarious situation, he felt something delicate like a flower climb up his arm, his shirt collar, his chin and from there up to his mouth. It was the little elf who had been forgotten in his shirt pocket and now with incredible difficulty she dragged along the magic pipe, which was six times longer than herself.

"Blow!" said the elf.

Knut felt the pipe in his mouth and began to blow. It sounded 'pu' again.

The spruce began to yawn, stretched out its branches and mumbled something about being disturbed in his afternoon nap. Whereupon he threw himself headlong down on the moss and in the fall crushed the great eagle beneath him. Knut crawled out from between the branches, heard the forest king snoring as if a hundred bears were humming in unison, and got back on his feet again as best he could.

'Now I must really look out for myself,' Knut thought. 'It is dangerous here in the woods; I had better walk along the shore path next to the sea.'

Soon he made his way over a heap of fallen logs to a fence, stepped over it and was on the shore path. He viewed the wide-open sea here, a far greater expanse than the narrow strait at Pärlebank. The west wind blew, not hard and furious as it often blows out at sea, but rather with that light, fresh breeze which sailors prefer as their ship dances along on the waves. And the little waves, with their rounded backs and happy leaps, chased after each other. They might have resembled frisky little children, splashing in the bathtub, if they had not been dressed in sea-green shirts and dresses, trimmed with fine white lace at the hems. Knut sat on a rock by the roadside. He felt tired and watched the waves. He had known them as far back as he could remember; he had grown up at the shore with them. Next to swimming in the waves, Knut knew nothing more enjoyable than to watch their merry antics. If only he wasn't so terribly hungry!

'If only I had all those flat stones I've skimmed along the surface of the water, and if they were real sandwiches, I could eat them all!' Knut thought to himself.

Then a wave rumbled so far up the shore that it splashed Knut's bare feet; out of the foam a white shoulder appeared and right away the loveliest little girl sat on the rock by Knut's side. She was almost as tall as he was, wearing light green clothing and silver bracelets, a gold comb in her long, golden hair and over it a wreath of the whitest water lilies.

"Good day to you, Knut Spelevink!' she said in a voice sounding as if a spring's source were murmuring amongst pebbles; "Why do you look so rundown today?"

Knut looked at her with amazement and replied: "Why wouldn't I look wretched, not having been offered any food since yesterday's lunch, other than a hot iron bar, frozen mercury, a drop of dew, a mosquito leg and seven loads of moss from the swamp?"

"Poor boy!" said the friendly little girl, stroking the hair from his forehead with her soft hand. "Come with me, and you will be able to eat your fill of sea foam and real pearls!"

"Thank you very much," said Knut; "but I would prefer a plate of fried flounder and fifteen sandwiches, spread with caviar[4].

The girl laughed. "Have you ever eaten our sea foam – like whipped cream with a heap of sugar on it? I'll tell you something. I am Undine Marina's dearest lady-in-waiting, and Undine Marina is the sea king's most beloved child. She lives in the beautiful coral castle over there in the sea and when she plays in the waves, she leaves her dainty footprints on the sand. Yesterday we played tag on the shores of Pärlebank, and Undine Marina dropped her magic pipe somewhere on the beach. The waves told me you have found the magic pipe. If you will come with me and give the pipe back to Undine Marina, you will be rewarded with a whole mountain of the sea's most precious pearls."

"I thank you, but no," said Knut, "I have been invited to Åsa for dinner and have not eaten anything since yesterday."

"Don't you think I'm beautiful enough?" said the mermaid, taking him with both hands and looking straight at him with her blue, twinkling eyes. "Don't you want to kiss my rosy lips?"

"You are not ugly", said Knut "but I would rather my lips kissed a good roast fowl."

"Listen to that!" said the mermaid with another resounding laugh. "I will tell you something else, Knut Spelevink! If you come with me and give the pipe back, you will be my most cherished fiancé, I will be your most beloved bride and we will live a thousand years blessed with silks and pearls."

"Well, I will tell you again!" replied Knut. "I have not eaten anything worth eating since yesterday and have been invited to Åsa for dinner. Goodbye to you, water nymph. Now I'm going on my way."

"You may swagger off," said the mermaid cunningly. "But you have no pipe."

"I don't have one?" exclaimed Knut, taking the pipe out of his shirt pocket. At the same moment he felt a great wave wash over his head and throw him back flat on the rock. He knew no more until he awoke, still on the rock, with the sun already in the west, so that it must now have been afternoon.

Knut rubbed his eyes and wondered where he was. There was Kiikkala forest with all its magic kings, where he had experienced so many adventures and been offered such outlandish breakfasts. There was the open sea, which continued to move in rippling waves towards the shore and splashed its foam all the way up to where he lay. But where was Undine Marina's lady-in-waiting? She was not to be seen; she had floated away with the backwash. And where was the magic pipe, where was the little elf, who had hidden in his shirt pocket and who so faithfully saved him from the golden eagle's claws? On the rock next to him lay an old broken piece of reed, but it would not produce a single note, and in his shirt pocket he felt a small wet spot, but if it was sea spray or remnants of the little elf which he had crushed to death against the rock, no one could tell. Knut began to suspect that he had gone to sleep in the sunshine and dreamt fantastic nonsense.

"Well, I am still invited to Åsa for dinner!" he exclaimed.

In a flash he was on his feet and set out to run the shortest way he knew right through the forest. That was not an easy task. The juniper bushes had a quarrel with his trousers, the spruce branches grabbed at his shirt, the blueberry twigs and heather undergrowth pecked at his bare feet. But Knut was determined to go forward, and he arrived at Åsa without further adventures, tired, hungry and red-faced, precisely at 4 o'clock in the afternoon.

"Welcome, Knut Spelevink!" said Mr. Peterman. "You look really cheerful today."

"Why wouldn't I look cheerful, having up to now only been offered a hot iron bar, frozen mercury, a drop of dew, a mosquito leg, seven loads of bog moss, a barrel of sea foam and a mountain of pearls?" said Knut.

"That is a lot of dishes in one day," said Mr. Peterman. "In this world, one should not think so much about food. When you constantly think about such things, you will meet the trolls, who prey on such people. Maybe you're hungry, my boy?"

Knut blinked sheepishly, clutched his hat between his hands and allowed that he hadn't quite starved to death.

"Well, I am glad," said Mr. Peterman. "I ate a late breakfast, and my people have not yet had time to pluck the birds. I trust you can wait until 8 o'clock, and then we will have supper."

'This is even worse than a hot bar of iron and seven loads of moss,' Knut thought to himself. But he bit his nails and replied that he could wait. "I'll have to think about the catechism," he said.

Mr. Peterman was a joker. He had been a poor boy himself and knew well enough what it was like to wait for four more hungry hours.

"Knut Spelevink," he said, "I notice now that you can do something else than think about food. Do you know that it takes courage to overcome oneself and forgo the very necessities to which we are attached in this world? I like you, my boy, I will take care of you, so that you can go to school and become a capable fellow. But what is that? I think I can smell roasting fowl. Step right in, my boy! Now you will sit at my own table and finally eat until you are really full."

'What is that?' That almost sounded like a catechism question. The doors to the dining room opened, a large, set table awaited, laden and fragrant with cooked food, ready for hungry guests. Mr. Peterman led Knut by the hand and Knut was allowed to sit at the table like a gentleman. He would have sat there to this day, he was so hungry, but long ago he took a piece of cheese home to his grandmother and was sent off to school.

Wipplustig

"Who wants to view my cabinet of wonders? Who wants to see the most remarkable thing in the whole wide world?" shouted Wipplustig[1]. He stood the cabinet on its four legs outside the gate, and everyone in the courtyard, big and small, old men and women, boys and girls, ran over, shouting, "Wipplustig is here with his wonder box!"

"Watch out now!" shouted Wipplustig. "Now the spectacle begins!" He turned a handle on the side of the cabinet, the front opened, a row of gaudy little dolls began moving across a stage. "Hats off, lads. Here comes Emperor Napoleon with his imperial eagle battle standard, his generals, field marshals and other ruffians. See how big he is, he is six inches tall, a head taller than the king of Spain and the courtiers. Beware, the soldiers are bringing their rifles to their shoulders; out of the way, boys, now it's going to be war! Trrrrum, the drums roll. Do you see the little drummer boy, who walks so straight, leading the emperor's guard in their bearskin hats? Isn't he brave? And the master trumpeter, there he blows down an entire regiment; follow that if you can! ... Here comes the English fleet, sailing on the sea... boom, the cannons roar..."

"My dear, can they roar a little louder?" asked old Kajsa in her red hat. "It's strange, I hear nothing, I think I've become stone deaf."

"Yes, I don't hear anything either," shouted Lat-Jakob, sitting down on the grass because he did not have a chair to sit on. "I have such big ears and still hear nothing."

"Pipe down please!" shouted Wipplustig. "How do you think you can hear the cannons when people are buzzing like flies around the cabinet?"

"I don't see nothing," sobbed little Greta, the crofter's daughter, who was no taller than a small broom, and stood behind Anders the tailor with his wide-shouldered, homespun jacket. "I can't see anything!"

"Hold your tongues!" shouted Wipplustig again. "I am telling you that now the English are coming, and boom, bam, if no one can hear the cannons, at least you can see them. Now little Napoleon with all his great army is wading into the water…"

"I don't see any water," cried Kajsa.

"Well, if you do not see the water, you will hear it," Wipplustig countered irritably. "Woosh, how the sea roars and the waves heave and the ships prepare for battle!... And now Emperor Napoleon grabs a ship of the line under each arm and saunters to the beach.

"I do not see any beach", shouted Anders the tailor.

"Quiet there! A small child could understand that the beach is behind the cabinet. Here come Turks, Tatars, Mamelukes, rabble-rousers, and other ruffians. Now they draw out their long sabres and start fighting. Crash, one cuts the head off another…"

"What's that?" Kajsa interjected, "Are they killing each other?"

"Send for the constable!" opined Lat-Jakob, lounging on the green grass.

"I'm scared, I'm so terribly scared," little Greta exclaimed, and then she started weeping.

"What is all this noise?" cried Wipplustig. "Settle down; let them kill each other in peace. Watch out, now something else is coming. Here, three tailors are walking along a road, bickering about which of them is the heaviest man. Shortly after them comes a farmer driving a cart. 'Do you have a weighing scale, old man?' 'Just a small steelyard balance, dear gentlemen.' 'That will work, bring it here.' So, these tailors get on the scale; one weighs one ounce, the second two ounces, the third three ounces. 'Yes, I knew that I would be the heaviest fellow,' says the one who weighs three ounces. 'No, wait,' shouts the farmer, 'remove the pressing iron and the thimble which you carry in your pocket!' Then the heaviest tailor is weighed once more, and then he weighs only half an ounce."

"That's not true," shouted Anders the tailor in his large homespun jacket. "That's not true, because those are just wooden dolls. A tailor is more than that. Have you not read about the valiant tailor who in battle struck seven with one blow?"

"Now we will see something grand," said Wipplustig. "Here comes the great Mogul and his court. He is hefty, he wears four bands, like barrel hoops, around his belly and all of them are of the purest gold. After him comes Mrs. Mogul, his mother, who is as thin as a straw, and after them the court trips along on tiptoe, for that is what happens at a court. There's going to be a dance: the great Mogul offers his arm to the Princess Sky Blue for a swinging reel. 'No, I thank you,' she says, 'I've got a splinter in my foot.' 'Never mind,' says the Mogul; then the musician plays a fanfare, and they dance. All of a sudden, one of the four golden bands breaks."

"No, now I'm going on my way," shouted Lena the shoemaker. "I can't follow this; he mixes it all up."

"Not to worry," said Wipplustig. "Here comes the goldsmith with his bellows and his tongs, he forges the gold band back together. Now the whole court is dancing the fandango. The giant Bumburrifex invites Princess Lindagull, and Knut Spelevink runs off with the Arabian king's one hundred wives, one under each arm."

"What's that?" cried Kajsa. "He takes one under each arm? How has he got so many arms?"

"He has them made from wooden skewers," Wipplustig replied. "Now everything is as it should be, but we have forgotten to invite the old man in the moon, who is usually the finest panjandrum at all weddings. All at once, he comes with an army of moon people…

"Are there people on the moon?" yelled Anders the tailor and leaned over the cabinet to see better.

"Of course," said Wipplustig. "On the moon it seems just like on earth, except that there is constant moonlight. It is also remarkable that on the moon everything is upside down compared to here on earth. Here you see the old man in the moon and all his people. They stand on their heads and walk on their hands. Try doing that, boys!"

"That's easy enough," shouted the boys.

"Now they enter the dance hall," said Wipplustig. "Do you notice how they wear big boots on their hands and hats on their feet? Four times four and forty thousand they are. Now they turn big Mogul and his whole court upside down…"

Crash ... the cabinet fell over on its back!

Wipplustig became furious. "Who has dared to overturn my cabinet?"

"Anders the tailor did that," Lat-Jakob replied. "Anders leant too far forward to see the moon people and pushed over the cabinet…"

"Oh no, that was part of the act; everything would be turned upside down," supposed Kajsa.

"Catch the scoundrel!" shouted Wipplustig. "Anders, Anders, the gold bands have fallen off Mogul, and his mother has been swept away!"

"Yes, grab him!" cried Lat-Jakob, stretching out in the grass. But Anders was already long gone.

"Listen, good people," said Wipplustig, "have you heard of the natural order? Now Anders has made an ugly break in the natural order. You see, I must go to the city and buy brass leaf for Emperor Napoleon's crown. Here is my hat; a coin for the old man in the moon will buy some darning needles for the masts of the English fleet! Like that, let them jingle! Thank you, good people! Don't worry about rewarding that organ grinder, it's just vulgar music, not worth a broken button. I will come again; I'm coming back with fourteen emperors. Farewell, old men and women! Goodbye to you, boys and girls! I'll be back next Wednesday."

Wipplustig went towards town with the cabinet on his back. Now the town was a good five miles or so, and before Wipplustig had reached halfway, the evening turned to dusk. It was not very dark, for the full moon shone brightly over the treetops. 'The night is beautiful,' thought Wipplustig; 'I will go to sleep here beside the country road.' And then he lay down with the cabinet for a pillow.

Wipplustig was tired, but he could not sleep, he thought the night sky seemed so vast and yet so close. 'It's quite peculiar,' he said to himself, 'how the moon looks at me with its big, chubby, cheese face. I can clearly see the old man and the old woman. They should thank me for inventing such a fantastic tale about them to amuse the simple-minded people.'

The old man and woman in the moon did not answer. It was quiet, so quiet in the sky and on earth. The great lantern of the night went its silent way over the blue vault and obscured the light of the stars.

It annoyed Wipplustig that the moon constantly looked at him and did not let him sleep. "Why are you staring at me?" he asked.

"Poor good-for-nothing!" said the moon.

"What's that?" exclaimed Wipplustig. "Why are you attacking me with abusive remarks? Am I not an artiste? Am I not the richest and most powerful man on earth? In my cabinet I have room for all the world's glory; armies and fleets obey my command, kings and emperors, I set them up and take them down at my whim and pleasure...'

"Wretched loser," reiterated the moon.

"No, that makes less sense than a brass button!" exclaimed Wipplustig. "Who can bear to hear such foolish talk? Look, there you are, North Star, almost right over my head. Don't let this insult go unanswered; rather tell the moon what kind of a man I am!"

"Jester," replied the North Star.

"Well, Twinkle Eyes, now you think you're smart. Ask the sun if my brass leaf is not just as good as her gold. But look, here flies an eagle ... Eagle, tell the moon and the stars what kind of a man I am!"

"You are a proper breakfast for me, worm," replied the eagle, who, swooping down on Wipplustig, hooked its claws into his torn sweater and lifted him high above the treetops.

"No, wait a minute," screamed Wipplustig. "Wait until next spring, I'm so skinny in the summer. Better still, over there in the village lives a tender tailor who is a fat lazybones. Dare I ask who my master is and where we are headed?"

"I am Emperor Napoleon's legendary eagle, and I am currently on a journey to the moon. I seek the emperor's crown, said to be in custody there."

"Well, that makes excellent sense," said Wipplustig. "Wouldn't I know Napoleon's crown? Give me freedom to travel back and forth to the moon, I have some friends there, we shall redeem the crown if it is in hock." Wipplustig thought to himself: 'I wish, Mr. Eagle, that you were nailed over our stable door in the village.'

"Let's go," said the eagle, extending its dark wings, rising above the clouds into the starry sky, and soon sitting, gasping for air, on the outer edge of the full moon. "Go now to redeem the crown!" commanded the eagle.

Wipplustig went; it was remarkably easy to walk about on the moon. He thought he could fly. It was a shiny gold land, with high mountains and deep valleys, but all upside down. The trees stood with their tops down and their roots up; the farmhouses were turned over with their chimneys against the ground.

'Who would have thought that I was just making this up?' thought Wipplustig. 'Now it remains to be seen if the moon consists of Dutch cheese.' He sat down, cut a piece of the ground and tasted it. "Yes, it really is Dutch cheese. A deep pit should be dug here," said Wipplustig.

No sooner had he taken up a generous piece of good cheese, before he saw a curious crowd was marching in the valley. It was an army of moon folk; everyone stood on their heads, walked on their hands and held their rifles between their toes. At the head of the army was the Man in the Moon himself. "Where is the scoundrel who said of us that we go around upside down?" commanded the Man in the Moon.

"Who would dare utter such a gross calumny?" Wipplustig asked trembling. "It's stupid to walk on your feet, when you have hands to walk on."

"You're the one who said it," roared the Man in the Moon. "Look at that dromedary, he walks on his feet!"

"Me?" said Wipplustig. "Certainly not. Why wouldn't I walk on my hands as nature intended?" And then he stood on his head but quickly tumbled to the ground.

"No," said the Man in the Moon, "you are good for nothing save as a jester to amuse my wife. She needs something to entertain her, poor old woman, since she has been stuck with her nose wedged in the moon mountain for a thousand years now. It was her punishment, as you know, when she tricked me into trying to tar the moon. She will not be freed until the biggest fool between heaven and earth comes here, and I confess that I would rather she stayed sitting there. She's way too neat and tidy, she'd sweep and clean the whole moon if she's freed one day. I like a little innocent mess, I have spilled ash from my tobacco pipe, a little here and a little there, it is fun to soil shiny scrubbed floors. When you amuse the old woman, make sure she does not get loose!"

"Forgive me," said Wipplustig, "I have to hurry back to Earth. I have promised Napoleon's eagle to redeem the emperor's crown."

"That toy?" exclaimed the Man in the Moon. "I have given it to my boys to play with. March to your appointed task, earth man!"

It was no use, Wipplustig had to march on his hands with the army and they all came to a large flamed coloured mountain where the Moon woman really did sit wedged in a crevice.

"Let me take a pinch of snuff." said the Man in the Moon, scattering snuff on the mountain. The Moon woman sneezed, the crevice opened, and the old woman was free.

"Well, in all my born days!" shouted the Man in the Moon. "The biggest fool between heaven and earth must be here. It can be none other than you, Wipplustig. Dear friends, let us now flee, for if there is now no lunar eclipse of rubbish and dust, it's only because there is no broom left in the kingdom of the moon."

The whole army made a hasty retreat. Wipplustig wanted to follow but was not yet well versed in the art of walking on his hands. He tumbled over, fell behind, got up on his natural legs and ran as fast as his trousers would allow. As he turned around, he saw behind him a large cloud of dust and heard the voice of the Moon woman: "Where are all the ants and worms that mess up my courtyard? It must be a clean house, a clean house in the moon's estate."

Before Wipplustig had time to count to fourteen, he had over him a swarm of people and things who fled from the broom. Everyone ran over him, pummelling and trampling him.

"Take that for my crown!" Emperor Napoleon shouted and pinched his ear.

"Here you have it for the darning needles in our battleships!" the English cheered and fired their cannons at him.

"Here you have it for my barrel hoops!" puffed the big Mogul and pinched him in the nose.

"Here you have it for taking me off so abruptly! "shouted the Mogul's mother and stabbed him in the cheekbone with a pin.

"Here you have it for the splinter in my foot!" cried Princess Sky Blue and hugged him half to death.

"There you have it for the weighing scales!" the three tailors shouted and singed him with their press irons.

"Here you have it for this, and there you have it for that!" shouted a hundred at once, and continued to bite, pinch, snap, and tug at poor Wipplustig, until his hearing and sight failed him. All this took place while fleeing, and shortly after all these torments came the old Moon woman with her immense broom. No one could escape it: she swept the moon as clean and shiny as a brass cauldron; all the rubbish was swept over the edge of the moon. Emperors, sultans, princesses, battleships, cannons, tailors, drummers, trumpeters, eagles, crowns and scales - everything swirled for a moment in the blue air and then was scattered like a shooting star at twilight.

Amongst all this rubbish swept away from the moon's disk was Wipplustig. He looked in vain for his eagle, he dangled down, he tumbled into open space, he fell and fell and fell - and woke up with an ant crawling in his ear. Where was he? On the forest hillside with his cabinet under his head. Morning had broken, but the full moon still looked at him, pale and wan, with its yellow-grey face. Truly, he could still distinguish the old man and the old woman, and with a sigh of relief he noticed no trace of the terrible broom. Apparently, the old woman was still wedged in the rock. Wipplustig did not have to consider himself the biggest fool between heaven and earth…

"This will be a good story for the simple-minded folk," he said to himself, as he hung the cabinet by its straps onto his back. "Where is there anyone like me, who in one night makes such incredible journeys? And someone dared to call me a poor good-for nothing."

"Poor good-for nothing!" said an echo in the forest.

"Is that you, mouthless maiden?" grinned Wipplustig. "Hardly a loser, all ingenious men are said to be careless at times. But to call such an artist as I am, a joker…"

"Joker!" repeated the echo.

"Listen here, scandalmonger, I know you have a talkative tongue, but I avoid all personal remarks. Do you want a place in my cabinet? Am I a joker? I, who in this cabinet present the world's greatest wonders, am I a person whom one can, with impunity, call a fool?"

"Fool!" said the echo.

"No, this is getting uncomfortable. I'm going to town. Less of your sauce, crow!"

"Saucy crow!"

"Shut up!"

"Shut up!"

"I give you good day."

"Good day."

Little Lasse

There once was a boy named Lars, and because he was so small, he was called Little Lasse. He was a brave lad; he wanted to travel around the world in a peapod boat. 'What's that?' you ask. Well, in the summer when the peapods grew green and long in the garden, Little Lasse crept into the pea patch along the gap between the rows, where the pea stalks grew high above the cap on his head. He broke off seventeen big peapods, the biggest and straightest he could manage. Little Lasse thought that no one saw him, and that was foolish, because (so some say) 'God sees everywhere.'

Then the gardener came walking with his gun on his shoulder and heard something rustling in the pea patch. "I think it's sparrows," he cried. "Shoo, shoo!" But no sparrows flew up, because Little Lasse had no wings, only two small legs. "Wait, now I'll load my gun and shoot the sparrows," said the gardener. Then Little Lasse became a little afraid and crawled out of the vegetable patch.

"Forgive me, dear gardener," he said; "I was seeking out some beautiful boats for myself."

"I will let it go this time," said the gardener. "But next time, Little Lasse, you must ask for permission to search for vessels in the pea patch."

"I will do that," Lasse replied, and then he was off to the beach. There he opened his peapods with a pin, split them properly and inserted small sticks for rowing benches. Then he took the peas, which were in the shells, and loaded them into the boats. Some of the shells were broken, some remained whole; and when all was ready, Little

Lasse had twelve boats. But they would not be boats, they would be big warships. He had three ships of the line, three frigates, three brigs and three schooners. The largest ship of the line was called Hercules, the smallest schooner was named Flea. Little Lasse put all twelve in the water, and they floated splendidly; no large ships could dance more proudly on the ocean waves.

Now these ships would travel around the world. The big island over there was Asia; the big stone was Africa; the little island was America; the little stones were Polynesia, and the beach from where the ships sailed out was Europe. The entire fleet set out and sailed far away to the different continents. The ships of the line sailed straight to Asia; the frigates travelled to Africa; the brigs to America and the schooners to Polynesia. But Little Lasse remained in Europe and threw small stones out into the lake.

On the shore of Europe there was a real boat, Pappa's own beautiful, white-painted rowing boat, and Little Lasse climbed into the boat. The peapod boats had already gone so far that they seemed like little blades of grass out on the lake. Little Lasse got the urge to travel to the various parts of the world himself. It had surely been forbidden by Pappa and Mamma, but Little Lasse had forgotten that. 'I will row just a little way out,' he thought. 'I will catch up with the ship Hercules near the coast of Asia, and then I will row back home to Europe.'

Little Lasse shook on the chain with which the boat was tied up, and remarkably the chain came loose. So Little Lasse freed the boat and was ready to row. He knew how, because he had rowed so often on the staircase at home, when he pretended the stairs were a boat and Pappa's big cane was the oar. But now when Little Lasse wanted to start rowing, there were no oars in the boat. The oars were stored in the boat-house, and Little Lasse had not noticed that the boat was empty. It is not as easy as one would think, to row to Asia without oars.

What would Little Lasse do now? The rowing boat was already a good distance out, and the wind, which blew from the land, drove him ever further out on the lake. Now Lasse became a little scared and started shouting for help. But there was no one on the beach; no one heard him. Only a big crow sat alone in the big birch tree; beneath the birch tree crawled the gardener's black cat stalking the crow. Neither cared the least about Little Lasse drifting out upon the lake.

Little Lasse now regretted that he had been disobedient and gone out in the boat, when his Pappa and Mamma had so often forbidden it! Now it was too late, now he could no longer get back to the shore. Maybe he would perish on the big lake. What could he do? When he had yelled himself hoarse and nobody had heard him, he clasped his little hands and said:

"Dear God, do not be angry with Little Lasse!" And then he fell asleep.

Although it was daylight, the Sandman[1] sat on the shore of Dreamland[2], fishing for small children with his long fishing rod. He heard the gentle words that Little Lasse spoke to God; at once he pulled the boat up to himself and lay Little Lasse down to sleep on a bed of roses.

Then the Sandman told one of the dreamchildren: "Play with Little Lasse so that he doesn't get bored!" There was a little dream-lad, so small, so tiny that he was smaller than Lasse himself; he had blue eyes, fair hair, a red cap with a silver ribbon and a white shirt with pearls on the collar. He came to Little Lasse and said: "Do you want to travel around the world?"

"Yes," said Lasse in his sleep, "I certainly do."

"Come on then," said the dream-lad, "and let's sail in your peapod boats. You sail in Hercules, and I will travel in Flea."

So they departed from Dreamland, and in a little while Hercules and Flea were on the shores of Asia, far away at the end of the world, where the Arctic Ocean flows through the Bering Strait into the Pacific Ocean. It was so terribly cold; the tall icebergs gleamed brilliantly, and the great whales that lived underneath could not knock holes in the thick ice with their large heads. All around the desolate beaches lay snow and more snow, as far as the eye could see; here and there small grey men, dressed in furry skins, drove small sleds drawn by dogs through the snow drifts.

"Shall we go ashore here?" asked the dream-lad.

"No," said Little Lasse, "I am very afraid that the whales will devour us, and the big dogs will bite us. I'd rather we travelled to another continent."

"Let's go," said the dream-lad with the red cap and the silver ribbon, "it's not far to America." And in the blink of an eye they were there.

It was sunny and very warm. The tall palm trees stood in long rows by the beach and bore coconuts in their tops. People, red as copper, galloped over the immense green prairie and threw their spears at the buffaloes, who faced them with their sharp horns. An immense king serpent crept up the trunk of the tall palm tree and threw itself down on a small llama, grazing on the grass at the base of the palm. Well, that was the end of the little llama.

"Shall we go ashore here?" asked the dream-lad.

"No," said Little Lasse, "I am very afraid that the buffaloes will gore us, and the great serpent will eat us up. I'd rather we travelled to another continent."

"Let's do it," said the dream-lad with the white shirt, "we have only a small distance to Polynesia." And then they were there.

Here it was even hotter, as hot as in the bastu[3], when you have just poured water onto the stove. Here, the most precious spices grew by the beach: bushes of pepper, cinnamon, ginger, saffron, coffee and tea. Brown people, with scarily painted faces, chased a yellow, striped tiger amongst the tall bamboo by the beach, and the tiger turned and struck his claws into one of the brown people. Then everyone took flight.

"Shall we go ashore here?" asked the dream-lad.

"No," said Little Lasse, "Don't you see the tiger over there in the pepper bush? I'd rather we travelled to another continent."

"We can do that," said the dream-lad with the blue eyes, "We don't have to go far to Africa." And as he said it, they were there.

They anchored at the mouth of a large river, and the shoreline was as green as the greenest velvet. A short distance from the river spread an immense sandy desert. The air was yellow; the sun was burning so hot, as if it wanted to burn the earth to ashes, and the people were black as the blackest ink. They rode through the desert on tall camels; lions roared with thirst, and the big crocodiles gaped up out of the river with their grey lizard heads and their sharp, white teeth.

"Shall we go ashore here?" asked the dream-lad.

"No," said Little Lasse, "The sun will burn us, lions and crocodiles will do us harm. I'd rather we travelled to another continent."

"We can sail back to Europe," said the dream-lad with fair hair. And with that, they were there.

They came to a beach. Everything there was so cool, familiar, and friendly. There stood the tall birch tree with its hanging branches; at its top sat the old crow, and at its foot crept the gardener's black cat. Nearby was a farmyard, which Little Lasse had seen before. By the farmyard was a garden, and in the garden was a pea patch where long peapods were growing. There the old gardener with his green cap was walking, wondering if the cucumbers were ripe. On the steps, Fylax was barking, and when he saw Little Lasse, he wagged his tail. Old Stina was milking the cows in the cowshed. An awfully familiar woman, in her plaid woollen shawl, was going to see how the fabrics were getting bleached on the green grass. A very familiar gentleman in a yellow summer coat, with a long pipe in his mouth, strode down to see how the harvesters were cutting the rye in the lower field. A boy and a girl ran along the shore and shouted:

"Little Lasse! Little Lasse! Come home and eat a sandwich!"

"Are we going ashore here?" asked the dream-lad, staring mischievously with his blue eyes.

"Come along, and I'll ask Mamma to give you a sandwich and a glass of milk." said Little Lasse.

"Wait a little," said the dream-lad. And now Little Lasse saw how the kitchen door stood open, and from there a slow, pleasant, hissing sound was heard, as when you pour the yellow batter with a ladle into a hot pancake pan.

"Maybe we should go back to Polynesia now?" whispered the happy dream-lad.

"No, now they are frying pancakes in Europe," said Little Lasse and wanted to jump ashore, but he could not. The dream-lad had tied him up with ribbons of flowers so that he could not move. And now all the little dreamchildren gathered around him, a thousand and more little cherubs, and sang a little song:

The world is so big, so huge,
Lasse, Little Lasse!
Bigger than you'd ever think,
Lasse, Little Lasse!

Lands are hot and lands are cold,
Lasse, Little Lasse!
But God's love is everywhere,
Lasse, Little Lasse!

Many people live there,
Lasse, Little Lasse!
Happy that God loves them all[4],
Lasse, Little Lasse!

When the angel of God goes with you
Lasse, Little Lasse!
No snake will bite you
Lasse, Little Lasse!

Say, where do you thrive the most?
Lasse, Little Lasse!
Away is good but home is best,
Lasse, Little Lasse!

When the dreamchildren had sung their song, everyone soared away, and the Sandman carried Lasse back into the boat. For a long time, he lay completely still, and he could still hear the rustling of the frying pan on the stove at home. The sizzling became increasingly sharp; Little Lasse heard it quite close beside him - and then he woke up and opened his eyes.

He still lay in the boat where he had fallen asleep. The wind had turned, and the boat that had drifted out with one wind now swung back to the shore while Little Lasse slept. And what Lasse imagined to be the sizzling of the frying pan was the slow murmur of the waves as they hit the pebbles on the beach.

Little Lasse rubbed the sleep from his eyes and looked around. Everything was as before, the crow in the birch tree, the cat on the grass and the peapod fleet by the beach. Some of the ships were wrecked, and some had drifted back to shore. Hercules had returned with her cargo from Asia; Flea had come back from Polynesia. And all the continents were exactly where they were before.

Little Lasse did not really know what to think. He had so often been in Dreamland's cave, and yet he did not know how dreams can play tricks. But Little Lasse did not trouble his head with such things; he gathered up his ships and marched up the beach back to the farmyard. Then his brother and sister came to meet him and called out:

"Where have you been all day, Lasse? Come into the house, and you'll get a sandwich!" The kitchen door stood open, and from there a familiar sizzling sound was heard.

The gardener was standing near the gate, and watered the dill, parsley, carrots, and parsnips. 'Well,' he said, "where has Little Lasse been all this time?"

Little Lasse stood up straight and replied: "I have sailed around the world in a peapod boat!"

"Aha!" said the gardener, doubtfully.

Epilogue

The gardener had forgotten Dreamland, hadn't he!

But you have not forgotten it, you know it exists, you know its glorious cave. The luminous silver walls never rust; the sparkling diamonds are never dim, and the soft, slow music plays unceasingly in the cave's lovely evening twilight. Just as the bright stars never age, so the light, airy dreamchildren in Dreamland's halls never grow old. Perhaps you saw a glimpse of the dreamchildren's delicate wings as they flew around your pillow? Maybe you have met the same dream-lad with blue eyes and fair hair, wearing the red cap with silver ribbon and a white sweater with pearls on the collar? Perhaps he also showed you all the countries and peoples of the world, the cold wilderness, and the scorching deserts, people of many different colours and the wild animals in the sea and the forest, so that you may learn about everything, but be glad to come back home at last? Who knows? Maybe you have also travelled around the whole wide world in a peapod boat?

A Winter's Tale about Skyhigh and Cloudbeard

Far away in Finland's great forest wilderness, there stood two tall pines very close to each other. They were so very old that no one remembered anymore when they had been young saplings. Now, their dark canopy towered high above all other trees, and they could be seen from far away. In the spring, the song thrush sang lovely melodies in their branches, and the small, pink, heather flowers looked up at them admiringly, as if they wanted to say: "How is it possible that anything could grow so tall and become so big and so old?" But in winter, blizzards covered the whole neighbourhood in snow and the grass withered and the heather flowers slept deep under the white blanket of the drifts. Then wild storms passed through the crowns of the pines and swept the snow from their evergreen branches; and a tempest might sweep away large houses and topple entire forests. But the pines stood steadfast and never wavered, nor did they break when everything else broke around them. Their strength was impressive.

Not far from these trees, one could see a hill in the forest, and on it rested a little cottage with two small windows and a roof covered in turf. A poor crofter and his wife lived there, and they had a potato patch and a small field close by their cottage. In the winter the crofter cut down trees in the forest and dragged the logs down to the big sawmill ten kilometres away, and by doing so he earned just enough to afford butter and bread and milk and potatoes. He and his wife thought that was fine, for many had to be content with bark bread[1] and certainly didn't have any butter to spread on it.

The crofter couple had two small children, a boy named Sylvester, and a girl named Sylvia. One wonders how they got such names; perhaps from the forest, for 'sylva' means forest in Latin. But Sylvester is in the almanac and is the last saints' day of the year; so that the boy had his name day every year on New Year's Eve.

Now it happened one winter's day - it was New Year's Eve - that both children went out to check on their traps in the forest, set up for catching hares and willow ptarmigan[2]. And behold, there was a white hare in Sylvester's trap and a white willow ptarmigan in Sylvia's. But both the hare and the ptarmigan were still alive, only stuck by their legs; and they began to whimper so pitifully that the children were astonished.

"Let me go, and you'll get something good!" said the hare. "Yes, release me and you will get a reward!" said the ptarmigan.

The children took pity on them and let them loose. The hare, as fast as he could, scurried off into the forest and the ptarmigan flew away as quickly as her wings allowed, and both shouted: "Ask Skyhigh and Cloudbeard! Ask Skyhigh and Cloudbeard!"

"What does that mean?" Sylvester said in annoyance. "The ungrateful beasts did not even say thank you."

"They both told us to ask Skyhigh and Cloudbeard," said Sylvia. "Who could they be? I have never heard such strange names before."

"Neither have I," said Sylvester.

At the same moment a sharp winter wind blew through the two tall pines very close by, and there was a murmur in their dark canopies, and the children heard strange words in the murmur.

"Are you still standing, Brother Skyhigh?" said one pine tree.

"Of course I'm standing," said the other. "But what about you, Brother Cloudbeard?"

"I'm getting old," replied Cloudbeard. "The wind broke off a branch in my crown."

"You're just a child compared to me," said Skyhigh. "Only three hundred and fifty years old, and I have turned three hundred and eighty-eight. Just a kid! Just a baby!"

"Now the storm is coming back," said Cloudbeard. "It would be good to sing a little, so my branches have something to think about." And so, they began to sing together in the storm:

Hear our words!

High in the north,

Long in time and deep in the earth

Our roots go down,

We stand our ground:

That is how we face the storm.

Winter's snow, summer's showers,

Centuries of shadow pass before our eyes,

Cloud father,

People are born and perish:

We still stand.

Human children, tender saplings,

Grow, as we, big and strong,

Rooted in fells and forest.

Grow in life's clamour to meet the sky,

Grow in light towards the embrace of God.

Grow with your forehead, like our canopy,

Raised high in the sky!

"Let's talk now to the human children," growled Skyhigh.

"I wonder what they intend to tell us," muttered Sylvester.

"No, come on, let's go home," Sylvia whispered. "I'm very scared of these tall trees with their strange songs."

"Wait, I see father coming with the axe on his shoulder," said Sylvester. The crofter arrived and said: "Well, I could make good use of these trees," he said. And he lifted the axe to cut down Skyhigh.

But the children began to cry. "Dear father, don't cut down Skyhigh!" pleaded Sylvester.

"Sweet, dear father, do not cut down Cloudbeard!" begged Sylvia. "They are so ancient and have sung a song for us."

"What a childish notion!" reckoned the crofter. "As if old trees could sing! But it is all the same to me; since you have pleaded for them, I will look for another pair of trees."

And he went further into the forest. But the children remained, curious to hear what Skyhigh and Cloudbeard would say to them.

It did not take long until the wind rushed back from the mill, where the millstones tumbled, and began to hiss again in the pines. Then the children heard quite clearly that the trees began to speak again.

"You have saved our lives," they said, "and it does you great credit. Now you can ask for a gift, and whatever you desire, we will give you."

The children suddenly became very happy but very perplexed. They thought they had nothing more to wish for in this world. Finally, Sylvester said: "I want there to be a little more sunshine, so we would see the hares' footprints on the snow better."

"Yes," said Sylvia, "and I want it to be spring soon so that the snowdrifts begin to melt and then the birds would start singing in the forest again."

"Foolish children," said the trees, "you could have wished for all the beautiful things in the world, and instead you wished what will happen anyway, regardless of your desires. But you have saved our lives, and therefore you will get your wishes fulfilled in a better and more beautiful way. You, Sylvester, will receive the gift that wherever you go and wherever you look, there will be sunshine around you. And you, Sylvia, will get the gift that wherever you go and wherever you open your little mouth, there will be spring around you, and the snowdrifts will melt. Is that good?" said the pines.

"Yes, yes," cried the children with much delight, "it's more than we asked for, and thank you, dear trees, for the good gifts!"

"Goodbye to you," said the trees. "Good luck!"

"Goodbye, goodbye," said the children and started walking home. As they walked, Sylvester often looked around, as he usually did, for ptarmigan amongst the trees, and behold, it was marvellous that wherever he looked, it seemed there was a ray of sunshine before him, shining clear and bright over the branches. Sylvia was no less astonished that the drifts began to melt on both sides of the footpath where they were walking. "Do you see! Do you see!" she cried to her brother, and she had scarcely opened her mouth, before the green grass began to spring up at her feet, and the trees began to bud, and the first lark was heard trilling high up in the blue sky.

"Oh yes, this is so much fun!" the children shouted and ran home with delight to their mother. "I can see sunshine!" cried Sylvester. "I can melt snow!" cried Sylvia.

"Well, anyone can," said Mother and laughed. But it wasn't long before her eyes were really opened. As the evening began to get dark, there was no darkness in the cottage, but bright sunshine, until Sylvester became sleepy, and his eyes slowly closed. And even though it was the middle of winter, there was such a scent of spring in the cottage that the besom[3] in the corner began to turn green, and the rooster became so delighted that he began to crow as evening fell. And that lasted until Sylvia fell asleep.

"Listen, Father," said Mother when the crofter came home. "There is something not right with the children. I'm afraid they've met a troll in the forest."

"You're just imagining it, Mother," said the crofter. "I have some news to tell. Can you guess what it is? Well, the king and queen are traveling through the country and will come past our church tomorrow. Why don't we go there with the children to see the royal couple?"

"Yes, I agree," replied the old woman. "It is not every day you get to see the king and queen."

The next morning the crofters and their children made their way to church in plenty of time and were so excited by what they would see that none of them thought of what had happened the day before. Nor did they notice how the sunshine radiated in front of their sleigh and how the birches budded around them on the roadside.

When they came to the church, they found many people gathered there, but all were worried and anxious. There was talk that the king was very displeased because he had found the land so desolate and wild, and since he was very austere, he blamed this on the people and would probably impose harsh punishments on them. It was also said that the queen felt the cold keenly here in Finland and was very miserable and melancholy throughout the journey.

Everyone knew this already, and so everyone trembled when the royal sleighs came like a whirlwind along the road. The king looked grim and the queen tearful, but they stopped awhile by the church as the horses were changed. They looked around, for the silver-plated convertible tops were folded down on the sleighs.

"Look at the beautiful sunshine all of a sudden," said the king and laughed quite graciously, just like ordinary people do. "I cannot understand why I suddenly have become so happy," he said.

"It must be because Your Majesty ate a good breakfast," the queen replied. "I feel the same way too."

"That must be because Your Majesty slept so well last night," said the king. "Anyway, just look how beautiful it is, this desolate Finland! See how the sun shines on those two tall pines over there in the forest! We should build a royal estate for ourselves here."

"Yes, let us do it, my lord and king," said the queen. "The climate must be mild in this area. Just see how the green leaves are appearing on the trees in the middle of winter!"

As they spoke, they became aware of Sylvester and Sylvia, who had climbed onto a wooden fence so as to be able to see the royals properly, and as Sylvia chattered with joy, the dry fence sprouted large green leaves around her.

"Look, there are two nice children," said the queen. "Let them come up to the sleigh."

The children came, with their fingers in their mouths, for that is the height of fashion on such occasions.

"Listen to me," said the king, "I like you; I've become quite warm and happy upon seeing you. Come with me in the sleigh, so that you can travel to our royal court, to be dressed in gold and fine clothes and make all our people happy."

"No thank you, Mr. King," Sylvester and Sylvia replied. "We would rather make our father and mother happy at home. And at the court we would get lonesome for Skyhigh and Cloudbeard.

"Is it not possible to take Skyhigh and Cloudbeard with you?" asked the queen, for she also felt so uncommonly warm around her heart.

"No thank you, Madam Queen," the children said again. "That would not work, since they grow here in the forest."

"What ideas these children get into their heads!" said the king and queen, laughing so much that the royal sleigh rocked. Then they gave the order to build a royal villa nearby and were so happy and gracious that everyone was amazed. All the poor received gold coins, and Sylvester and Sylvia also received the large royal pretzel, which the court baker baked for the trip, and which was so large that it had to be pulled by four horses. And the children shared the pretzel with all the children in the village and still had so much left over that the crofter's horse could barely drag home all the pretzel pieces.

On the way home, the crofter woman whispered to her husband: "Do you know why the king and queen were so happy?" "No," said the husband. "Well, it was because Sylvester and Sylvia looked at them. Do you remember what I said yesterday?" " Hush," said the husband, "do not tell the children about it. It is better that they are not aware of their wonderful gifts which are beyond human understanding."

And with all the excitement over the large royal pretzel, Sylvester and Sylvia forgot that they could make sunshine and melt snow. They weren't aware of how happy and warm all the people became when they saw them; and since they were good and kind children, everyone thought that was the cause. It was certainly true that they were a delight to their parents and that the whole wilderness around the croft was gradually transformed into rich and beautiful arable fields next to green pastures, where, most unusually, the birds of spring sang all winter long. After a few years, Sylvester became a forester at the new royal estate, and Sylvia managed the large garden. It was remarkable that everywhere these children looked, everything thrived and flourished.

One day Sylvester and Sylvia came to visit their old friends Skyhigh and Cloudbeard. As before, a wild winter storm blew, and it whistled and roared in the high dark crowns of the pines, and the trees sang an old song again:

Aha! Aha!

We are so old, we are so grey,

But big and strong in the storm we stand,

Hundreds of years,

In autumn and spring,

In winter cold,

In summer showers,

In frost and snow,

In rain and thaw,

In night and fog,

At dawn and dusk;

Aha! Aha!

We are so old, we are so grey,

But big and strong….

And just as they got this far in the song, a crick and a crack, and a crash were heard and both Skyhigh and Cloudbeard lay shattered side-by-side on the ground. Skyhigh had reached three hundred and ninety-three years of age, and Cloudbeard was three hundred and fifty-five. They had not noticed how eventually their roots had withered and rotted so that the relentless winds prevailed against their strength.

But Sylvester and Sylvia gently patted the moss-covered trunks of the dead pines and spoke such loving words to them that the snow melted all about and the pink heather flowers grew everywhere around the fallen trees. And so, the grave of Skyhigh and Cloudbeard was marked with flowers.

It's been a long time since I heard anything more about Sylvester and Sylvia, and they have probably already become old and grey themselves, since it has been many years since a king and queen travelled through Finland. But every time I see two good, happy children, loved dearly by all, then I fancy that they must be Sylvester and Sylvia, and that they got their merry eyes from Skyhigh and Cloudbeard. Not so long ago, I saw two such children, and it was remarkable that wherever they looked, a ray of sunshine radiated in front of them and shone over the cloudy sky and over people's sad or indifferent faces. The children themselves did not know this, but it was impossible to see them without becoming as wholeheartedly glad as one gets when one sees innocence, joy and goodness in the world. Then the ice on the window and the drifted snow begin to melt, as does the frost in the frozen hearts of men, and it becomes spring and green amid the cold winter, so that the broom in the corner begins to get green leaves and the dry fence blossoms into roses and the larks sing high in the heavens. For all this, we must thank Skyhigh and Cloudbeard and be grateful to the good Earth when the joy of verdant spring returns each year.

Sampo Lappelill

This story takes place in Lapland long ago. In the far north of Sweden, Norway, and Finland, you won't see any fields and regular houses nor any real forest, but only large, desolate bogs and high mountains. The Sámi[1] live there, a nomadic people living mostly in small lodges. Their country is a wonderful place. Half the year it is almost constantly bright, since the sun never sets in the middle of summer, and half the year it is almost constantly dark, so that the stars shine all day in winter. For much of the year it feels like winter, and the Sámi men and women ride across the snow in a sleigh, called a pulka[2], pulled by a reindeer. Have you ever seen reindeer? They are the size of a small grey horse, with high branching horns and a beautiful small head with big bright eyes. And when they run, they take off like a snowstorm over mountains and hills, their hooves clacking. The Sámi love galloping with their reindeer and pulka, and they wish there could be such good sleighing all year round.

There was a Sámi man and woman who lived in the far north of Lapland in a place called Aimio, close by the great river Tana[3]. You can find this at the very top of a map of Finland, where Lapland looks like a large, white nightcap on Finland's high head. This place is desolate and wild, but the Sámi man and woman certainly believed that nowhere on earth would you find such white snow and such clear bright stars and such magnificent northern lights, as there in Aimio. There they had built a lodge in the traditional style. Trees did not grow in their area, except for small, slender birches, which looked more like bushes than trees; one wonders where they got enough timber for their lodge. Nonetheless, they found narrow, long poles and pushed them down into the snow and tied them together at the top end. Then they hung reindeer skins over the poles, so that everything looked like a grey sugar loaf, and thus their lodge was finished. At the top of the sugar loaf, they had left a hole through which the smoke escaped when they lit a fire in the lodge, and there was another opening on the south side, through which one could crawl in and out. This is what the Sámi lodge looked like, and the Sámi thought it was splendid and warm and they felt good in it, even though they had no bed or floor other than the white snow.

The man and woman had a little boy called Sampo, a name which signifies[4] happiness and good fortune in Finland. But Sampo was so privileged that he had two names; one was not enough. Once, strangers in large fur coats had come there and rested in the lodge. They brought with them hard, white pieces of snow, called sugar, which the Sámi woman had never seen before. They gave a few pieces of the sweet snow to Sampo and patted him on the cheek and said: "Lappelill[5]! Lappelill!" They could not say anything else since none of them could speak the Sámi language. When they left to travel further north to the North Cape and the Arctic Ocean, the Sámi woman, who liked the strange gentlemen and their sweet snow, began to call her son 'Lappelill'.

"I think Sampo is a much better name," said Pappa somewhat annoyed. "Sampo means wealth, and I tell you, Mamma, do not discredit his name! Our Sampo will become the king of the Sámi and rule over a thousand reindeer and fifty Sámi lodges. You shall see, Mamma, you shall see!"

"Yes, but Lappelill sounds so sweet," said Mamma. And so she called the boy Lappelill, and Pappa called him Sampo. But you should know that the boy was not baptized yet, for in those days there was no pastor for 200 miles.

"Next year we will go to the pastor and christen the boy," Pappa would say. But the next year was challenging, and the journey was abandoned, and the boy remained un-baptized.

Sampo Lappelill became a small chubby boy of seven or eight years, with black hair, brown eyes, a snub nose, and a wide mouth, just like Pappa himself, and in Lapland he was considered handsome. Though young, Sampo was an active lad; he had his own little skis, with which he danced down the high slopes by the Tana river, and his own little reindeer, which he strapped to his own pulka. You should have seen how the snow swirled around him when he whizzed around on the ice and through the high drifts, so that there was nothing visible of the boy other than a small tuft of his black hair.

"I will never be at ease until the boy is baptized," said Pappa. "The wolves could take him on a beautiful day out there on the fells. Or he might encounter the goblin Hiisi's reindeer with the gilded horns, and then God have mercy on any poor man who is not baptized!"

Sampo heard those words and began to wonder what kind of reindeer could have gilded horns.

"It must be a magnificent reindeer," he said. "I should have this reindeer drive me to Rastekais!" Rastekais is a very high and desolate mountain, fifty or sixty miles beyond Aimio.

"What nonsense you talk, you reckless boy!" scolded Mamma. "The trolls are right at home on Rastekais and Hiisi also lives there."

"Hiisi, who is that?" asked Sampo.

The woman was embarrassed. 'So, the boy catches on quickly!' she thought to herself. 'Why do I talk about such things in his presence? But it would be good for him to be afraid of Rastekais.' And so, she said:

"Dear Lappelill, never go to Rastekais, because Hiisi, the great mountain king, lives there. He can gobble a whole reindeer in a single mouthful and devours little boys like mosquitoes!"

At these words, Sampo looked very thoughtful, but kept quiet. To himself he thought: 'It would be amazing indeed to get to see a giant like the mountain king - but only from a distance!'

It was already three or four weeks after Christmas, and it was still very dark in Lapland. There was no morning, noon, or evening, only constant night, and the moon shone, the northern lights crackled, and the stars burned brightly all day long. Sampo found it boring. It had been so long since he had seen the sun that he had almost forgotten what it looked like, and when someone talked about the summer, Sampo did not remember anything; only that summer was when the mosquitoes were so nasty and really wanted to just eat him up. Therefore, thought Sampo, the summer might as well be gone forever, since the white snow made it light enough to travel about on skis.

One day at noon (although it was dark) Pappa said: "Come here, you should see something!" Sampo crawled out of the lodge and looked to the south, where Pappa was pointing. There he saw a small red streak on the horizon.

"Do you know what that is?" asked Pappa.

"It's the southern aurora," said the boy. He was well aware of the points of the compass and knew that one could not see the Northern Lights in the south.

"No," said Pappa, "it's the sun's harbinger. Tomorrow or the day after, we may see the sun itself. Just look at the extraordinary red glow shining on top of Rastekais!"

Sampo turned to the west and saw in the distance how the snow was coloured red on the dark, gloomy peak of Rastekais, which he had not seen in a long time. Again, he thought how terribly exciting it would be to catch a far-off glimpse of the mountain king.

Sampo pondered the matter all day and half the night. He wanted to sleep but could not. 'My,' he thought, 'it would be altogether extraordinary to see the mountain king just once!' He thought and thought, until finally he crawled quietly out from under the reindeer furs where he lay, and out through the doorway of the lodge. It was so cold, the stars sparkled, and the snow crunched underfoot. But Sampo Lappelill was not a pampered lad and was not troubled in the least. What's more, he wore a leather jacket, leather pants, Sámi fur-boots, a leather hat and leather gloves. So equipped, he looked at the stars and wondered what he should do next.

Then nearby, he heard his little reindeer scratching in the snow. 'What if I were to ride a little?' wondered Sampo. No sooner said than done, Sampo harnessed the reindeer to the pulka, and glided off swiftly over the wide, desolate, snowy landscape.

'I will ride a little way towards Rastekais, just a short distance,' he thought to himself. And he went off across the frozen river and then up on the other bank of the Tana, and then Sampo was in the Kingdom of Norway since the Tana river forms the border. But Sampo did not know that.

Sampo Lappelill, riding with his reindeer over the snow, sang to himself and his reindeer:

"The day is so short,
The road is so long,
Run along with my song,
Let us hurry away!
There is no peace here,
Only wolves live here."

And when Sampo sang, he saw the wolves running like grey dogs in the darkness around the sleigh and snapping at the reindeer, but Sampo did not care. He knew well that no wolf was as nimble on its feet as his good reindeer. How they flew over hills and rocks as the wind whistled around his ears! Sampo Lappelill just let the reindeer go. 'Click-clack' sounded its hooves, the moon in the sky ran along with the reindeer, the high mountains seemed to run backwards, and Sampo Lappelill just let him run. It was fun to ride, and that was all he thought about.

Then on a short turn down a hill, the sleigh tipped over and Sampo fell out and lay in a snowdrift. But the reindeer did not notice and, thinking that Sampo was still sitting in the pulka, kept running, while Sampo, his mouth full of snow, could not shout 'Whoa! Whoa!' (or whatever call is usually used for reindeer). There he lay like a helpless lemming in the middle of the dark night, amid the vast, immeasurable wilderness where no one lived for miles around.

It would not surprise you that Sampo was a bit alarmed at first. He crawled out of the snowdrift unhurt but that alone wouldn't help him much. As far as he could see in the pale moonlight, all around him there were only drifts and fields of snow and high mountains. But one mountain rose high above all the others, and Sampo realized that he was now near Rastekais. Suddenly it occurred to him that the cruel mountain king lived there, who could eat a whole reindeer in a single mouthful and could swallow little boys like mosquitoes. Then Sampo Lappelill became afraid. Alas, how he longed to be home again with Pappa and Mamma in their warm lodge! But how would he get back there? And before he could get far, wasn't the mountain king likely to catch him and devour him, trousers and gloves and all, just like another wretched little mosquito?

Sampo Lappelill sat there all alone in the snow and darkness amid Lapland's deserted mountains. It was so strange and frightening to see the high, black shadow of the Rastekais mountain in front of him, where the mountain king lived. He started to cry but that did not help at all, for all his tears instantly froze and fell like icy peas down onto his little shaggy reindeer jacket. Sampo realized it was pointless to cry and got up from the snowdrift and jumped around to keep warm.

'If I stay here, I will freeze to death,' he said to himself. 'No, I'd rather go to the mountain king. If he is going to eat me up, he eats me up. But I want to tell him that he should rather eat up the wolves on this mountain. They are meatier than me, and he would have less trouble with the fur.'

Then Sampo set out to climb up the high mountain. He had not climbed far before he heard a pitter-patter in the snow and a great shaggy wolf leapt up beside him. Sampo's little Sámi heart skipped a beat, but he decided to pretend he was not the least bit scared.

"Don't get in my way!" he shouted to the wolf. "I have a message for the mountain king and watch out for your hide if you mess with me!"

"Well, well, what haste," said the wolf, for on Rastekais all animals can speak. "Who are you, little pixie, roving around in the snow?"

"My name is Sampo Lappelill," the boy replied. "And who are you?"

"I am the mountain king's chief great-wolf," replied the beast, "and I have been running around the mountains to summon his people to the great sun feast. As you are going the same way as me, you can sit on my back and ride up to the mountain."

Sampo didn't hesitate; he climbed on the wolf's furry back, and they galloped off over ravines and precipices.

"What do you mean by 'sun feast'?" asked Sampo.

"Don't you know?" said the wolf. "After the whole long dark winter here in Lapland, when the sun first rises again above the horizon, we celebrate the feast of the sun. Then all the animals and all the trolls in the whole of the Nordic countries gather on Rastekais, and on that day no-one is allowed to harm another. That is your good fortune, Sampo Lappelill; for otherwise, you see, I would have eaten you a long time ago."

"Does the same law apply to the mountain king as well?" asked Sampo.

"Of course," said the wolf. "An hour before sunrise and an hour after sunset, the mountain king himself would not dare to touch a hair on your head. But beware, when the hour is over, if you are still on the mountain, then a hundred thousand wolves and a thousand bears will rush towards you, and the mountain king will seize whatever he can get hold of, and it will soon be over for Sampo Lappelill."

"Perhaps you would be so good as to help me get home again, when it will be so dangerous to travel?" Sampo asked with a trembling heart.

The wolf began to laugh (because at Rastekais the wolves can laugh). "Never imagine that, dear Sampo!" he said. "On the contrary, I will be the first to grab you. You're a strong, chubby boy, your flesh filled out with reindeer milk and reindeer cheese. You will taste splendid for early morning breakfast."

Sampo wondered if it wouldn't be best to immediately jump off the wolf's back, but it was now too late. They had already reached the top of the mountain, and there you saw something amazing. The great mountain king sat on his throne of soaring cliffs and gazed far out over the mountains and valleys covered in night. On his head he wore a hat of white snow clouds; his eyes were like the full moon as it rises over the forest; his nose was like a mountain peak; his mouth was like a ravine; his beard was like a tuft of long icicles; his arms were as thick as the largest pine in the mountains; his hands were like spruce boughs; his legs and feet were broad like winter toboggan runs, and his wide coat was like a mountain of snow. But if you ask how one could see the mountain king and his people here in the middle of the night, you should know that the snow gleamed all around, and across the heavens shone the most brilliant aurora, which illuminated the area. Around the mountain king sat millions of mountain trolls and elves, some as grey and small as a squirrel. They had gathered here from the ends of the earth, from Nova Zemlya and Spitsbergen and Greenland and Iceland, even from the North Pole itself, to venerate the sun. These savages worshiped the evil being out of fear, for the trolls did not like the sun at all and would rather it never rise again once it had sunk behind the desolate mountains. And further away stood all the small and large animals of Lapland in long, dense rows, thousands and thousands, from the bear, the wolf and the wolverine, all the way to the gentle reindeer, the modest lemming and the nimble reindeer flea, but the mosquitoes were unable to attend - they had frozen to death.

Sampo Lappelill saw all this with much astonishment, stepped down unnoticed from the chief wolf's back and hid behind a large rock, to see what would happen next.

The mountain king raised his head high as the snow swirled around him and the bright northern lights shone like a halo around his forehead. The aurora went out in long, star-shaped, pale red rays over the blue night sky; it crackled and it hissed, as when a fire in the forest winds its way up into the crowns of the pines; it expanded and contracted; it brightened and faded, so that one flash of light after another flared over the snowy mountains. And this amused the mountain king. He clapped his icy hands, so a roar like thunder echoed in the mountains, and the trolls squeaked with joy, and the animals all around screamed in terror. But this amused the mountain king even more, and he cried out across the wilderness: "That's how it should be! Eternal winter and eternal night! I like that."

"Yes, so shall it be!" shrieked the trolls loudly, for they all liked the night and winter much more than the summer and the sunshine.

But among the animals a loud murmur arose, for though all the predators, and the mountain rats as well, thought like the trolls, the reindeer and the others favoured the summer, even if they did not immediately remember the mosquitoes of Lapland. The little reindeer flea much preferred summer, and therefore it squeaked as loudly as it could:

"Your Majesty, we have come here to wait for the sun!"

"Will you keep quiet, you lousy bug!" roared the polar bear next to it. "We only gather here because it's an old custom. But this year it will be fun, this year the sun will be gone forever. The sun has gone out, the sun is dead!"

"The sun has gone out! The sun is dead!" muttered all the animals, and there was a shudder throughout nature. But the trolls from the North Pole laughed so hard that their hats flew off. And the great mountain king raised his thunderous voice, and roared again over the wastelands:

"That's how it should be! So shall it be! The sun is dead. The whole world will fall down and worship me, the king of eternal winter and night."

This annoyed Sampo Lappelill, where he sat behind the big boulder. He stepped forward and shouted with bold impudence:

"You're lying, mountain king, you're lying, you know you are! Yesterday I saw the harbinger of the sun in the sky, and the sun is not dead. Your beard will still melt when midsummer comes."

At these words, the mountain king's forehead darkened like a black cloud, and he forgot the law and raised his terrible long arm to crush Sampo Lappelill. But at the same moment the northern lights faded, and a red streak sprang up in the sky, and shone into the mountain king's frosty face, so that he suddenly became dazzled and let his arm fall. And then one saw a golden ribbon of sunlight rise slowly and majestically over the edge of the horizon and illuminate the mountains, the wastelands, the drifts, the gorges, the trolls, the animals and the little courageous Sampo Lappelill. Suddenly there was a shimmer in the snow, as if many millions of roses rained down over it, and the sun shone into everyone's eyes and down into everyone's hearts. Even those who had most rejoiced that the sun was dead now were sincerely glad to see it again. It was comical to see the trolls' amazement. They glared at the sun with their small, grey eyes under their red nightcaps and against their will were so delighted that they stood on their heads in the snow, and the big, terrible mountain king's beard began to melt and drip down into a flowing stream over his wide jacket.

But while the multitude took diverse delight in the sun's return, the first hour was almost gone, and Sampo Lappelill heard one of the reindeer say to its little reindeer calf:

"Come, come, dear child, now we must go, for otherwise we will be eaten by the wolves!" Then Sampo remembered what was ordained if he were to delay any longer. And when he saw beside him a splendid reindeer with large, gilded horns, he did not hesitate but jumped up on the reindeer's back, and they went off at a full gallop down the mountain's slopes.

"What is that strange pounding I hear behind us?" Sampo asked after he had caught his breath a little during the frantic ride.

"It's the thousand bears lumbering after us to devour us," replied the reindeer. "But do not be afraid! I am the mountain king's own enchanted reindeer, and no bear has yet nibbled at my heels."

So, they rode again for a while. Then Sampo asked:

"What is that strange panting I hear behind us?"

The reindeer replied:

"It's the hundred thousand wolves that race after us to tear you and me apart. But do not be afraid! No wolf has ever caught up with me in the mountain wilderness."

Having rode for a while longer, Sampo Lappelill then said:

"I wonder if there is a thunderstorm in the mountains behind us?"

"No," said the reindeer, who began to tremble all over, "it is the mountain king himself who treads with giant steps after us, so now it is all over for both of us, for no one can escape him."

"Is there no way out?" said Sampo.

"Not really," said the reindeer, "our only possible salvation is to try and get to the church over by lake Inari. If we get there, we are saved, for the mountain king has no power over Christians."

"Yes," said Sampo, "run, my kind-hearted reindeer, over mountains and fields, and I will give you golden oats to eat from a silver manger!"

And the reindeer ran and ran for dear life, and just after they entered the pastor's cottage, the mountain king was already in the yard behind them, pounding so hard on the door that everyone thought the whole house would fall to pieces.

"Who's there?" said the pastor.

"It's me!" replied the thunderous voice out in the yard. "Open up for the mountain king! Here is an unbaptized child, and all the pagans belong to me."

"Wait a minute, until I get my cassock and my collar on, so I may receive such a noble gentleman with dignity," replied the pastor inside.

"Get dressed," roared the mountain king, "but hurry up, otherwise I will kick down the walls of the house."

"I'll be quick, gracious lord!" replied the pastor. But at the same moment he took a bowl of water and baptized Sampo Lappelill as a Christian, in the name of God the Father and the Son and the Holy Spirit.

"Well, are you not ready yet?" roared the mountain king and lifted his fearsome foot to topple the house down. But then the pastor himself opened the door and said:

"Get thee hence, O king of night and winter, you have no more dominion over this child! The sun of God's grace is now shining over Sampo Lappelill, and he no longer belongs to you, but to the kingdom of God!"

The mountain king was so outraged that he burst forth in a terrible snowstorm, and it began to snow so heavily, so thickly, that the snow went all the way up to the roof of the pastor 's cottage and snowdrifts hid all the graves in the churchyard. The pastor stayed calm and read prayers from the Holy Book and waited for dawn. And when morning came, the sun shone on the snow, and the snow melted away, and the pastor 's cottage was saved. The king of the mountains had disappeared, and no one knows for sure, but all believe that he still lives and reigns on Rastekais.

Sampo Lappelill thanked the good pastor and borrowed a pulka from him. Sampo harnessed the reindeer with golden horns to the pastor 's pulka and went back home to his Pappa and Mamma in Aimio. And there was great joy when Sampo Lappelill came back so unexpectedly. But how Sampo then became a great lord, who fed his reindeer with golden oats from a silver manger, is another story, too long to tell now. It is said that from that time forth the Sámi no longer delay but every year bring their young children to be baptized, for who would like to see their child eaten by the terrible mountain king? Sampo Lappelill knows what this means. He knows what it is like when thunder is heard in the mountains.

The Waterlily

Were you ever over there on the small island in summertime, where the beautiful birches sway in the wind and where the water is so very clear that you can see the ruffe[1] swimming over the white sand? If you were there, you probably saw the big grey rock by the shore and the white waterlily at the foot of the rock; she, who as evening came, drew herself together and hid her flowers under her green leaves. Many thought she was betrothed to the sun, for very early every morning she opened her clear flower-eyes again and looked up, so snow-white and innocent, at the light in the heavens. But Waterlily was not so presumptuous that she could think of such a distinguished fiancé, who stood so high up above her and, moreover, was so much older than she, that she did not even dare to call him 'Uncle'. No, she did not aim so high. She had become good friends with the young birch tree which stood closest to the shore, trailing its long dangling curls over the water, where Waterlily was spread out on the surface, never swimming away from her roots.

Waterlily was not only beautiful, but she was also kind and humble, a winning combination. That's why everyone liked her, and so it came about that she had suitors, a whole battalion. There was a company of bulrushes not far from her, and one of the bulrushes constantly bowed to her, whenever the smallest gust of wind passed over the lake. "Your most humble servant," said the bulrush to her and bowed so deeply that it almost touched the water. But Waterlily did not like such strait-laced humility, for she noticed that the bulrush usually would be harsh and haughty towards the little roaches which swam around it and did their pirouettes in the sunshine. There was another suitor whose back was even stiffer, and that was a pole by the shore, where the old fisherman used to fasten his nets, lest the waves should wash them away. The pole stood bolt upright and never moved out of the way either for people or beasts, and so was often in a quarrel with one or the other if they came too close to it. Waterlily did not like that either, for she was meek and conciliatory and did not like to argue with anyone, not even with the old rowing boat which, when taking a hasty turn, paddled right over her.

The third suitor was a large outcrop, known as a boundary-stone because it marked the border between two villages. On beautiful days, when the sun shone, the boundary-stone became quite warm in its stone heart, as it stood and admired Waterlily; but it was so terribly old, more than six thousand years, and moss grew throughout its crevices. Waterlily had an awful lot of respect for the boundary-stone, but it couldn't be said that she wanted to marry it. That would have been pushing respect too far. In truth, Waterlily was sweet on the young green birch, which always nodded so kindly to her when it gazed upon the water, and it did that almost too often, but that was because it saw its reflection in the watery mirror encompassing the white maiden, its little waterlily.

I have forgotten to say who Waterlily really was. She was the youngest and most beloved child of the old Necken[2], and he had rocked her in his arms when she was little, and he often still lifted her on his broad shoulders when he emerged from the depths in the clear morning waves. And when evening fell and the sun sank into the sea and Waterlily hid her white crown under the leaves, then the old Necken sang his songs for her, and she rocked gently, very slowly in the swell, until her eyes closed, and she dreamed bright summer dreams of everything beautiful on earth.

"Do not get too close to me, you old sea ghost!" growled the pole at Necken. But the bulrush, which was always ready to ingratiate itself with the nobles, bent over in a graceful bow and constantly whispered: "Greatest respect to your Excellency! Your most humble servant!"

"Do not bother about those fools," said the boundary-stone to Necken, for they were old acquaintances. "You can bring your little girl up here to me, she will feel like a pearl in gold," said the boundary-stone.

"Now I've heard everything!" said Necken and laughed, so that the water swirled around his beard. "Yes, it would suit you perfectly to move my white flower up into your mossy nest!"

"Why!" said the boundary-stone, "what does it matter if I am a few thousand years old? At least I am steadfast and mature and do not blow away with every gust of wind, like those other clowns."

"No," said Necken, "put those foolish fancies aside, and let us remain good friends."

But the boundary-stone, the pole and the bulrush had become convinced that one of them should indeed have the white waterlily for its wife.

One night the boundary-stone awoke to find the young, extravagant southwest wind lying asleep at the foot of its crag and said to it: "Since you have taken your night's lodging with me, it is only fair that you do me a favour."

"What would that be?" said the southwest wind.

"Well, when the sun rises tomorrow, you should blow with all your might, so that you blow down the green birch tree there by the shore, for it is on his account that Waterlily never wishes to be my wife."

" I'll do that," said the southwest wind. "I have broken cedars and palm trees like match sticks; why couldn't I topple a puny little birch?"

The bulrush, on the other hand, spoke to the sea waves, which came in a sleepy, gentle swell through the strait. "My gracious sea troll, I am your most humble servant," it said. "Please do me a little favour in passing."

"Well, what would that be?" yawned the waves.

"Please rise up on the beach over there and knock down that green birch! It is on his account that little Waterlily never wishes to be my wife."

"Very well," said the waves. "I have washed away forests and cities; it's a small thing for me to sweep away such a little birch sapling. But now I'm sleepy; we can wait until tomorrow for that task."

"Much obliged," said the bulrush.

The pole also meant to harm the birch and undertook to quarrel rather slyly with the fisherman, who just that evening tied his nets to it.

"You pillory post," said the fisherman angrily, "Will you stop tearing my nets?"

"Is it my fault that I'm so gnarly?" replied the pole. "Nearby is a birch which would suit you much better. Chop him down tomorrow and stick him in the water."

"You may be right," said the fisherman. "I will think about doing that in the morning."

So the evening passed, and it became night, and Waterlily closed the white petals around her white crown, and the birch stood quite green with delight as it gazed at her in the beautiful twilight of the first night of August. Neither of them suspected any evil, and Waterlily slept like a good child. A large yellow moth, which had heard what the rock, bulrush and pole were planning, fluttered anxiously around the birch, but the birch did not notice it. It had other things to do. It washed itself in the dew which rained in small clear pearls over it and thought only of being especially charming and handsome when the water lily opened her innocent flower eyes again.

Eventually, a red streak appeared in the northeast sky and the whole neighbourhood began to brighten. The red streak grew redder and brighter, until the entire northern and eastern skies were on fire and the clouds seemed to be burning.

The fisherman woke up and looked out of the window of his cabin. "Oh no," he cried in amazement, "Looks like we will be getting a severe storm today; I'd better hurry out to salvage the nets."

But it was still quite calm, so tranquil that not a single green curl of the birch was ruffled in the cool morning air. Waterlily began to open her closed crown and, with sleep in her eyes, greeted the birch with 'good morning'. She had never seen the birch so elegant and charming, and never had the birch seen her so especially adorable. They were so cheerful and gay at heart, and just at that moment the sun rose behind the red clouds and looked affectionately upon them in their young innocent happiness in the early morning hours.

Then the boundary-stone impatiently shook its overnight guest, the wild southwest wind, which snored in the soft grass. "Don't just lie there, get to work!' said the rock.

"Leave me in peace!" replied the southwest wind, straightening its large, cloudy wings, which it spread over itself like a blanket. But the rock gave it no peace. "Well, then I'll fly and make the air whistle in your ears," said the southwest wind, annoyed and drowsy, and with one leap it was up in the air, roaring through the treetops.

That morning it was in a particularly wild mood, that crazy southwest wind. It was not long before the sky was darkened by its immense wings and white foam began to froth over the surface of the sea. But the birch and the waterlily did not yet notice anything amiss. They amused themselves by sending affectionate greetings to each other with a small, gilded dragonfly, which flew over the water from one to the other.

The storm increased. It swooshed in the trees, it stirred up the sea and it crashed around the rocks, as if a hundred thousand kittens were at war with a hundred thousand puppies. The waves began to rush in through the strait, so that the little humble bulrush became wholly ill at ease as it bowed and twisted in a thousand ways before the wind.

'Maybe it was foolish of me to beguile the sea troll just here,' the bulrush thought to itself, but it was too late to regret that now. Already it saw in the distance a whole mountain of water and foam rolling towards the strait. "There it comes, there comes my wave!" shrieked the bulrush in terror. And the mountain of water rolled over the bulrush and tore it loose from its roots, and its last words were: "Your humble servant!"

The troublesome pole did not fare any better. It tried to stand firm and struggled for the longest time, firmly shouting "none of your insolence" at the waves. But when the great sea wave came, it was all over for the pole. 'Ratsch', it broke in two and was flung far away amongst the foam and breakers.

The boundary-stone, which had seen so many storms in its time, stood completely safe despite all this ruckus and laughed in its stony heart at the destruction all around. It did not notice that the southwest wind, in its frenzy, had awakened the majestic thunder that slept in the clouds. 'Ritsch', a long, jagged, terrible lightning flashed across the whole arch of the sky, hit the rock and split its thousand-year-old stone heart in two, and there the boundary-stone lay, sundered.

Old Necken had much to do at home that day, for the waves rushed so furiously over the silver roof of his coral castle that he was kept busy nailing down the roof tiles. But when evening came and the boisterous southwest wind flew towards the sun and settled down (for the southwest wind usually never calms down by itself), then Necken ventured out of his castle to look for his little, beloved, white lily. He found her with her delicate stalk broken and her white crown crushed at the root of the birch tree, but one could still see on her snow-white cheek and her beautiful, faded leaves, that she had been broken in her moment of bliss, when her young flower heart was full of peace, joy, and innocence. Then the old Necken wept, his tears fell as big as sparrows' eggs into his long beard, and he buried the Waterlily in the earth at the root of the birch tree. And the birch wept, so that tears rained down from its locks. and the gilded dragonfly wept so much that it washed away its golden eyes and became blind; and the dew wept until the whole meadow was wet, and the bright evening sun wept beside the clouds, until a magnificent rainbow arched over the green forest.

But the boundary-stone could not cry, even if it had a desire to, for it was split in two, and the bulrush lay withered at the foot of the crag. The old fisherman searched for his pole in vain and thought briefly about chopping down the birch tree to make a new one, but then he thought it was a shame to damage such a beautiful tree and left the birch standing. A decent thought, don't you agree?

Next spring, there may be a new water lily at the foot of the birch, next to the island's shore. It's the dead Waterlily's little child, and we'll see if it's as beautiful and innocent as its mother.

Adalmina's Pearl

A fairy tale

Once upon a time there was a King and a Queen who had a daughter called Adalmina, a princess of course. Since she was her parents' only child, they doted on her dearly[1]. When Princess Adalmina was baptized, two good fairies, one red and one blue, were invited to be godmothers; that's the fashion for royalty in fairy tales. And the two good fairies did not forget to each give the little Princess a christening present.

The red fairy gave her a large genuine pearl, so incomparably beautiful that its match had never been seen, and from this, three more good gifts followed. "You should know," said the red fairy, "that as long as Adalmina carries the pearl with her, she will remain beautiful, rich, and wise. But if she loses her pearl, then forthwith she will forfeit the three gifts: her beauty, her wealth, and her wisdom. She will not get them back until she recovers her pearl again."

Well, that was clear enough. The blue fairy said: "Adalmina has received three gifts so grand that many can't imagine wishing for anything better. Nevertheless, there is another gift, the very best, and I give it to Adalmina, but only on one condition. As long as the Princess possesses her pearl and the three gifts, then my gift has no power at all. But if she loses her pearl, and her beauty, wealth, and wisdom, then she will receive from me in return the fourth gift, and that is a humble heart." Well, just as clearly said. And both fairies nodded farewell and disappeared like two white clouds in the blue summer sky.

The King and Queen were very pleased. They thought to themselves: 'If our little Princess will be beautiful, rich and wise, it matters little what her heart is like. We should take good care of her pearl, and then she can do without the blue fairy's meagre gift. No, the red fairy knew better what a princess needs! Her gifts were royal gifts, but the blue fairy was rather stingy, one must admit; she gave our dear child an alms token, just as one throws a copper coin to a beggar girl on the country road.'

Now the King had a gold crown made which fitted exactly on little Adalmina's head, and which was so constructed that as the Princess grew bigger, the crown got bigger at the same time and fitted as well as before. But for everyone else, the remarkable crown was either too big or too small. At the top of the crown was a setting, and in this the pearl was mounted so firmly that it was impossible for it to fall out.

Then the crown was put on Adalmina's head, and she wore it constantly, both when she slept in her little gilded cradle and when she was awake and running around the castle. But because the King and Queen, her parents, were so afraid of losing the pearl, it was strictly forbidden to ever let the Princess go farther than to the great gate between the King's courtyard and the park; and she was constantly followed by four chamberlains and four ladies-in-waiting when she went out, and the servants had strict instructions to carefully guard the Princess and her pearl. They dared not allow themselves to be careless, for the grim, red-clad executioner with the ugly beard and the terrible executioner's axe would not excuse any foolishness.

That's how the Princess grew up, and things turned out exactly as the red fairy had predicted. Adalmina became the most beautiful princess ever seen, so beautiful that her little eyes shone like two bright silver stars on a spring evening, and wherever she went, there was sunshine around her, and all the flowers in the garden bowed to her and said: "You are more beautiful than us!" And she became so very rich that it seemed as if treasures grew around her. The floor in her room was made of silver and mother of pearl; the walls were filled with large mirrors, and the ceiling was of gold, studded with diamonds; how it sparkled in the light of the lamps! Adalmina ate on gold, slept on gold, and clothed herself with gold; yes, if it had been possible to eat gold, she would have done it, but it was a little too hard to chew. And she was so very wise that she could guess the most difficult puzzles and remember the lengthiest homework, even if she only looked at her lessons once; and all the wise men in the kingdom came together to ask the Princess questions, and all agreed that such a wise and prudent princess as Adalmina had never existed in the world before and never would exist again for as long as the world spins.

Well, that was all well and good; it is no sin to be beautiful and rich and wise, if one understands that one should use these gifts to benefit mankind[2], but therein lies the difficulty. The King and Queen thought in their delight that Princess Adalmina was the best and most perfect being on earth; and the misfortune was that Adalmina began to think the same. When everyone constantly told her that she was a thousand times more beautiful and richer and wiser than other people, she gladly believed them, and so she became arrogant in her heart, such that she considered everyone else, even her parents, to be inferior to her. Poor Adalmina. It became a big, ugly stain on the lustre of her beauty. There was a great poverty in all her wealth, there was a great folly in all her wisdom, and thereby she was close to being completely lost.

For the older she grew, the more arrogant she became, and pride engenders the most unpleasant faults, so that Adalmina also became mean and hard-hearted, greedy, and envious. When she saw a beautiful flower in the garden, she hurried to trample it with her foot, for no one else but she alone was allowed to be beautiful. When Adalmina met another princess, riding in a gilded carriage, she was indescribably upset, for no one other than Adalmina was allowed to be rich and noble. And if it was said of another girl that she was kind and intelligent, Adalmina wept bitter tears of anger, for why should anyone else also be wise? Adalmina scolded all who did not flatter her and who would not let her do as she wished; yet she despised most of all those who were most submissive to her will. She was a tyrant, whom everyone feared, and no one liked; the King and Queen were the only ones in the kingdom who did not resent her pride.

One day, when the Princess was fifteen, she went out for a walk in the King's courtyard. When she came to the gate and wanted to go out into the park, she found the gate was locked, and no one dared defy the King's strict ban and open it. The four ladies-in-waiting and four chamberlains were in attendance but for the first time, they refused to obey the Princess' command. Then Adalmina became angry, so enraged that the sunshine of her beauty was completely darkened. She slapped her faithful servants in the face, ran away from them, and climbed over the gate. When the servants followed, she ran farther and farther into the park, until she lost sight of the servants amongst the green trees.

Then, for the first time in her life, Adalmina felt thirsty and tired and sat down by a spring to rest. Yes, she allowed herself to scoop water from the spring with her nice white lady's hand and drink just like other people do, when no one curtsies and offers them a glass of water on a tray. At the same time, she became aware of her image reflected in the water. "Oh, how beautiful I am!" she said to herself, and she tilted her head lower and lower towards the water to get a better reflection, until 'splash', the entire golden crown with the pearl fell off Adalmina's head and disappeared like an stone into the rippling mirror of the spring's water.

Adalmina was so captivated by her own beauty that she hardly noticed. But quickly, the water of the spring became still and clear again and Adalmina saw in its mirror a completely different image of herself. She no longer saw the beautiful Princess in her gold-knit dress, with jewels in her hair and earrings of glittering diamonds; she saw only a poor, unsightly, beggar girl, bareheaded, barefoot, in torn clothes and uncombed hair. In the blink of an eye, all her great wisdom also disappeared; she became as ignorant and foolish as the most uneducated person, and it was strange that at the same moment she completely lost her memory, so that she no longer knew who she was and where she came from and where she intended to go. She only vaguely felt that some great change had taken place, and it frightened her so much that she ran away from the spring and ran farther and farther into the forest, not knowing where she was headed.

As evening fell, it became dark and the wolves in the forest began to howl. Adalmina became more frightened and ran faster and farther, until she saw a light glowing in the distance. She came to a small cottage and found an old, poor woman living there.

"Poor child," said the old woman, "where have you come from, so late in the evening?" But Adalmina could not answer that. She no longer knew who she was and where her parents lived. The old woman thought this very strange, took pity on Adalmina and said to her, "Since you are so poor and alone in this big old world, I will let you live here with me. I really need someone to shepherd my goats in the forest. You could do that, my child, and if you are kind-hearted and modest, and happy to eat bread and water with a little goat's milk sometimes, then that will be like a feast."

Adalmina was very pleased with all this and kissed the old woman's hand with heartfelt gratitude. For without the girl knowing it, the blue fairy had kept her word: Adalmina had now acquired a gift better than beauty and wisdom and wealth, namely, a good and humble heart. She was much happier now, as she guarded her goats and ate her meagre bread and slept on a hard bed of straw and moss. She was much better off now than before, for with a humble heart many precious gifts, such as a good conscience and quiet contentment, peace and tranquillity, goodness and love, will follow wherever one ends up in the world. And wherever Adalmina went, again sunshine surrounded her, reflecting not her transient outer beauty, but the quiet aura that shines around the good and pious on earth, whose souls radiate beauty like the faces of angels when they, with their great white wings, descend into the valleys of this world.

But in the King's court there was a terrible uproar when the Princess disappeared. It helped little that the wretched ladies-in-waiting and the horrified, half-mad chamberlains who had followed her past the gate were thrown into a dark prison tower, where neither sun nor moon shone on them and where the red executioner with the ugly beard stood by the door with his axe. The King and Queen's grief was inconsolable, and they decreed that their entire kingdom be dressed in mourning. It was announced in all the churches that whoever could restore Princess Adalmina to them would be rewarded with the Princess as his wife, together with half the King's kingdom.

This was standard procedure in those days but nevertheless a good finder's fee, and many princes and knights wanted to earn it. For three long years they rode out across the wide world, winter and summer, and searched and searched, but never found even as much as the gilded heel of Adalmina's shoe. Finally, it came to pass that the young and dashing Prince Sigismund of Frankland, during his quest, came to the old woman's hut. There she sat in her widow's weeds, which were not elegant but were black, and the goats themselves on the stony hill were black and white.

"Who are you mourning, dear mother?" asked the Prince.

"The King has commanded that everyone should mourn our missing Princess," replied the old woman, "though it was no great loss to me. Certainly, she was beautiful and rich and wise, but people say she had an arrogant nature, and that's too bad for on account of that, no one really liked her."

Just then, Adalmina came home with her goats from the forest. The Prince looked at her and could not understand how a girl, who was so poor and unsightly, could still touch his heart so wonderfully that he was devoted to her before he saw more than the tip of her ear. He asked her if she had seen the Princess. "No," said Adalmina.

"It is remarkable," said the Prince. "For three long years I have not thought of anyone but my little Princess. But now I'm not looking for her anymore. Now I will build a castle for myself here in the forest and live here all the rest of my days."

No sooner said than done. The Prince built himself a castle, and it was right by the spring where Adalmina had been transformed in the past. Then one day, when it was very hot, the Prince became thirsty and leaned down to drink from the spring. "What could it be that shines so brilliantly down there in the water?" he said to himself. "I want to see what it is."

The Prince bent down, stuck his arm into the spring water and brought up a golden crown with a superb, beautiful pearl at the top. Then he remembered something. Imagine if it were Adalmina's pearl! Whereupon he went with the crown to the King's castle, and as soon as the King and Queen saw the treasure, they both shouted at once: "Adalmina's crown! Adalmina's pearl! Alas, where is she, where is our beautiful, dear little Princess?"

Then the King calculated that if the Princess was still alive, she would be eighteen years old. He remembered the red fairy's prophecy and began to surmise that it was the second part of the prophecy that had come to pass. Thus, the king proclaimed in the churches that all the girls who were eighteen years old should gather at his court and try on the crown. Whomever the crown fitted perfectly would be recognized as the true, lost Princess, and Prince Sigismund of Frankland would have her as his wife.

Of course, all the girls immediately hurried to the King's court; and those who were more or less than eighteen years of age pretended not to remember it. It was a beautiful summer's day, and at least a thousand girls stood outside in long lines, trying their luck. From early in the morning until late in the evening, the golden crown was passed from head to head and was tried on everyone but did not fit anyone. At last, all the girls began to grumble and say: "The King is making fun of us; let us draw lots, and the winner should be given both the crown and the Prince." Prince Sigismund thought this was rather dreadful and asked them to wait until the sun had set. "As you wish," said the girls.

Shortly before the sun went down, a guardsman was put on watch to see if anyone was still coming along the highway. The Prince shouted: "The evening advances, guardsman; do you see anyone coming along the road?"

The guardsman said: "I see the flowers inclining their crowns towards sleep, for the night is near. But I see no one coming along the road."

Again, the Prince asked: "The evening draws on, guardsman; do you see no one coming along the road?"

The guardsman said: "A cloud passes over the setting sun, and the birds in the forest hide their heads under their tired wings. The night is very close, and I see no one coming along the road."

Once more, the Prince asked: "The evening has ended, guardsman; do you not see anyone coming along the road?"

The guardsman said: "I see a small cloud of dust far away at the forest edge. Now it's getting closer; I see a poor shepherd girl pushing her goats in front of her on the road."

"Let us try the crown on the shepherdess," said the Prince. The other girls, who all considered themselves much better than her, shouted: "No, no!" But the King had the shepherdess brought forward, and behold, when they tried the crown on her head, the crown fitted perfectly. At the same time the sun set, and it became dark, so that one could not really see what the shepherdess looked like. But Prince Sigismund thought in his heart: 'Behold, the good God (or Fate) intends me to take this poor girl as my wife, and I will do so, for I have seen her before with the old woman in the forest and I know how it glows like sunshine around her wherever she goes.'

And all the people shouted: "Long live Prince Sigismund and Princess Adalmina!" But many thought to themselves: 'She's just a poor shepherdess!'

Then the shepherdess with the crown on her head was brought into the King's hall, which shone with thousands of candles. But Princess Adalmina's marvellous beauty shone brighter than all the thousands of lights when she finally stood in the middle of them all, dressed in her golden attire. For when she regained the pearl, she also recovered all the gifts of the red fairy. But the best thing was that at the same time she was allowed to keep the gift of the blue fairy, the good humble heart. And when she also recovered her memory, she remembered well what an unpleasant nature she had shown in the past, and how she was then transformed, and how the poor and the unsightly are much happier, untroubled by their conscience, than the rich and the beautiful with all their pride.

Because of this, she fell on her knees before her father and mother and begged them and everyone else to forgive her former arrogance. And as proof of how her heart had now changed, she brought the poor old woman out of the forest and embraced her, saying: "The charitable are rich despite their poverty, but the rich who have a hard heart know failure and distress amidst all their treasures."

And everyone who witnessed it could hardly believe their eyes. But

Prince Sigismund said: "I knew that's how it would be. Adalmina's pearl is very beautiful, but more beautiful yet is a humble heart."

Then there was a wedding and great joy in the King's court, and the four ladies-in-waiting and the four chamberlains were freed from the tower, and the red executioner with the ugly beard put his axe back into its closet, and all shouted throughout the kingdom: "Adalmina's pearl is wonderful, but a humble heart is far more precious!"

The Water Nymph's Footsteps

Over there by the shore, under the steep, forested hillside, have you seen how the tide etches its contours upon the white sand? The wavy lines go out in countless undulating bands to the low tide mark. Often when I see the big, white, foamy waves rushing furiously against the beach, it seems strange to me that they do not completely sweep away the twisted folds of sand. But the opaque waves just let the bands flex and fold in the sand as they storm and roar over their designs, before laying down again to rest in the depths.

The delicate stripes in the sand are the footsteps of the little waves, and the little waves are the curly-haired children of the sea, romping and frolicking on the soft sandy seabed. Every time a storm rages, the king of the sea says to his wild waves: "Go against the rocks, go up to the cliffs! But over there on the soft sand my little children play; no one is allowed to disturb their tracks and trails, no one is allowed to sweep away their footprints from the shore."

Deep down in the sea is the king's castle with its walls of crystal, windows of pearl and roofs of the most beautiful mussel shells. The king's sons and daughters, the blue waves, live there, as does his youngest and brightest little water nymph, the blue-eyed, silver-curled Undine Marina.

When Undine Marina goes out to play on the beach, she draws these fine wavy lines on the sandy floor with the tip of her silver shoe, and no heavy wave is allowed to obliterate them. Thousands of her brothers and sisters race with her there, and they all draw the same footsteps, but none of her siblings show such limpid and sinuous beauty as the lissom Undine Marina.

When the fishermen swim off the sandbank in the hot summer and the white seagulls fly like glistening stars overhead, then Undine Marina dances playfully about them, tumbling and curving in front of the sailors' boat and jumping around the young men who swim in the sunshine. But when the sun rises early in the morning from the ocean's bed, and again when she goes to rest at evening time in the forest, then Undine Marina sends ripples very slowly towards the shore and sings a long, melancholy song about times long gone, and friends who have long since passed on from us into the eternal silence.

Undine Marina had a dear friend, the little dark-haired Florio, the youngest of the princes of the forest. His green tunic was always adorned with many roses, his pockets were filled with nuts, and his brown cap bore an eagle feather. Florio often came to the beach where Undine Marina played, and soon they became very good friends. Often, they tussled playfully; Florio would throw twigs and pebbles at Undine Marina, and Undine Marina would sprinkle a wave over Florio's velvet boots in response. Then Florio would laugh, like the forest laughs when the leaves rustle, and Undine Marina would laugh, like the waves chuckle when the wind flies in their fluttering curls. But in the evening calm they played as if fiancé and fiancée; Florio sat on the grass by the beach, and Undine Marina leant calmly against the sandy seabed, and both told tales in turn. Florio knew how to tell both dark and light stories: about the trolls of the forest, snuffling behind the tall spruces, about the lion hunting in the dark moonlight and about the westerly wind's pranks with lilies of the valley in the meadows. Undine Marina told of centuries past, when the waves of the sea swept over all of Greater Finland, and of the giant cauldrons in the hills near the shore, and of the great whale that pulled her father's chariot through the coral forests in the mile-deep ocean.

Over the years they spent much time together each evening at the beach, and yet they remained little children, for the sons of the forest and the daughters of the sea do not grow up like human children. They live for many thousands of years, as long as the earth, and that's how they remain childlike and have so much fun in the evening twilight. And they liked each other very much, indeed so much that the white seagull which constantly saw them playing on the seashore used to say to its neighbour, the great sea eagle: "Florio and Undine Marina will surely become a couple, and then we will take part in the magnificent wedding."

"Yes, though it will depend on whether the wedding will be in the forest king's castle," said the eagle. "If it is with the bride's parents deep down on the seabed, then I'd be thankful for the invitation but could not have the honour to attend."

"Well, I didn't think of that," said the seagull. "But, when necessary, I know the art of diving, and it could be that I'll show up, because there will surely be many good fish dishes for supper on the wedding night."

That's what was said about Florio and Undine Marina. Then one evening, the king of the sea came riding on his big whale to the shore, where his daughter, the little princess, was telling tales to the forest prince. Now the forest and the sea were not very good neighbours, for they quarrelled over their borders and accused each other of illegally removing pieces of the other's land. For this reason, the sea-king became angry when he saw Prince Florio speak so amicably with Undine Marina, and the king threw a great wave towards the shore, which drenched the prince's fine green velvet tunic with mud and snatched the eagle feather right out of his hat.

Undine Marina sank distressed to the depths, and Florio turned with indignation back to the forest. But when his father, the king of the forest, heard how his beloved boy had been insulted, he was greatly outraged and sent out a multitude of terrible sandstorms, which filled in the whole bay with gravel, so that it became a large expanse of dry land and the sea king lost part of his territory. Of course, the sea king became even more enraged by this and sent out huge tidal waves, which flooded the forest, swept away the trees and tore off large pieces of the mainland and buried them under the waves. And so, there was a great, long, war between the sea and the forest because of Florio and Undine Marina, and the war continues even today when the two kings are in a bad humour. In between such times there is a truce, and then the waves go gently once more towards the shore, and you can still see Undine Marina's footsteps in the fine white sand in the evening twilight.

But now, Florio and Undine Marina can only seldom meet, in greatest secrecy, to tell each other the old tales and play together in a beautiful ring dance with the other small waves. Undine Marina often swims alone towards the beach, and you can sometimes see her white neck when the sunshine breaks through the dark clouds. Then you often hear her sing a lonesome song in the evening, and he who knows how to interpret the language of the waves can hear how she seeks her friend, who has gone away. "My charming lad has departed," she croons; "Long gone is the joy we shared at the beach; slowly I'll fall asleep here on the cushions of the sand. The friendship of sea and forest is severed; the dark spruce raises his crown towards the sky, and never, never can he descend to the sea's dark depths. But I see him nevertheless, I see him every night, and his tall crown is reflected in my blue eyes."

Do not grieve, my dear heart; trust that benevolent Fate[1] shall one day unite those who have long been separated, and the day shall come again when Undine Marina swims with joy to the shore and Florio seeks her footsteps in the silver-white sand in the calm of the evening.

Roaring Waters and Sighing Streams

"There's something strange about this brook," Richard said. "It seems as if it has something to tell me. Every time I dam it with a few stones, to make deeper water for my ships, it splashes water in my face and murmurs and babbles, as if it wanted to say: 'Listen now! Now listen!' Well, who knows, when it speaks a language that no one understands."

"Do you know," said Rosa, "It is just like that with my brook. When I paddle in it and wash the dolls' clothes, I think I see someone looking out of the water, nodding to me and saying to me: I know something you do not know!"

"That's because you see your own reflection in the water," Richard said.

"Like I did not think of that already!" said Rosa, annoyed. "But I tell you, the girl in the brook is a different girl from me, it's like we are sisters. When I open my mouth, she opens her mouth, but when I say something, she stays silent."

"It's the water-sprite's little girl," said Richard. "Be careful. If she's takes after her father, she will grab you by the leg and pull you into the water."

Rosa did not answer; she was offended.

"Now Rosa, don't be upset," said Richard. "Your brook and my brook are so close to each other that they surely flow from the same source. They must be sister and brother. My brook is bigger and stronger than yours, and he sometimes roars so fiercely when in the mood. That is why he should be called Roaring-Water."

"My brook is smaller and more gentle," said Rosa. "She sighs and murmurs so sweetly when the evening is quiet, and that is why she should be called Sighing-Stream."

"That's great!" said Richard. "Roaring-Water is my brother, and Sighing-Stream is your sister. It's fun when both have names."

"You know," said Rosa, "It's just as if Roaring-Water and Sighing-Stream were two small children. I wonder where they're going when they run out from here?"

"They go out into the big wide world," Richard said. "Come on, let's go and follow the streams to see. You walk along the banks of Sighing-Stream, and I will walk along the banks of Roaring-Water, and when we have pursued them both to the end, we will turn around."

"Yes, just wait while I run home for a sandwich," said Rosa. "Fetch one for me too!" said Richard.

After a while, Rosa came back with the sandwiches. "Bye to you," she said. "Bye, bye," said Richard. And so they both went to their respective brooks, Richard to Roaring-Water and Rosa to Sighing-Stream.

But now our saga becomes two stories, one about Sighing-Stream, the other about Roaring-Water. Which one should we hear first? How about Rosa and the Sighing-Stream?

Rosa went and spoke to the brook: "You little child, still in your cradle, what in the world will become of you? Flow quietly and gently, my beloved waters, and then show me your destiny, when you grow up!" Rosa walked and walked, and the brook flowed calmly and splashed her clear water on the flowers along her banks. Underneath, she drank the juices of the meadows and ate from the roots of the flowers and gradually grew larger. And the bigger she got, the clearer and calmer her water became, the more melodious her murmurs became, and the greener her banks became. Eventually she tumbled into a mirror-clear lake. There were birches and flowering rowan trees all around, and the sun in the sky looked down onto the calm lake, and snow-white swans swam around in the radiant splendour of the afternoon's golden hour.

Then Rosa clapped her hands and said to the brook: "You are so fortunate, my beloved little brook! All along your way you have spread blessings and greenery around you, and when your course is run then Mother Nature[1] lets you sink deeply into the embrace of the clear lake in the evening's blush. Let my destiny[1] be to also live and die like my little brook."

Then Rosa turned back grateful and happy, and got home again before nightfall. Richard had not returned yet. "He's coming, surely," said Rosa.

But Richard did not return. He did not come back that night, or the next day. Many years went by, and he did not return. 'Poor Richard,' thought Rosa; 'he had no more than a sandwich for the journey!'

In the end, everyone thought that Richard was gone forever, and everyone grieved a lot over that. Only Roaring-Water and Sighing-Stream roared and sighed plainly on summer evenings: 'Just wait, just wait, he's coming back!' But no one believed them.

So times passed, and Rosa grew up and forgot to wash the dolls' clothes in the Sighing-Stream and forgot to nod to the little girl in the brook, who once had been her best friend. Eventually, she had almost forgotten to mourn Richard; so many other thoughts came which obscured the memory of what had been long ago. But still Sighing-Stream and Roaring-Water murmured: 'Don't doubt he will come, yes, just wait, he will come back all right!'

And then one day a strange gentleman with a long black beard came and asked the young maiden in the garden about a child named Rosa. Now the girl he asked was Rosa herself, but she did not answer, she was embarrassed and shy. She could not understand what the unfamiliar gentleman was doing here.

Then the stranger became very despondent and said: "No one knows me here anymore, and Rosa, my sister, is gone now. I will go to the Roaring-Water and Sighing-Stream and ask them about my sister Rosa."

Thereupon, Rosa realized that the stranger was her own long-lost brother Richard, and it wouldn't have taken much to fly into his arms, saying to him: "Don't mourn, Richard, here I am, your very own sister, and now we shall never part again!" But she held back and said: "Come, let's go to the brooks!"

So they went, and between the brooks was only a narrow meadow, overgrown with the greenest grass. "Yes, I recognize my Roaring-Water," said the stranger. "Strange lass, do you want to hear my brook's story?"

"Yes, tell it to me," said Rosa, her heart beating loudly. And Richard began: "I was quite small, when I left my sister and my home, to see what would become of the brook when he grew big. From the beginning, Roaring-Water was fierce and wild, like an unruly boy, and would not permit any obstacles in his way. When he met a stone, he could be seen frothing with anger, rolling the stone away; but if there was a boulder in the way, then both fought for dominance, and most often the boulder won. However, the further Roaring-Water went, the bigger he became; smaller streams and rivulets poured their water into his, and so he became a river."

"I kept following his course, and when I got hungry, I asked for food at the cottages by the river, and when I got thirsty, I drank from the river, and when I fell asleep, I slept in the grass on the soft riverbank. Meanwhile, Roaring-Water became even bigger and wilder. Now he no longer made way for boulders; he flowed over them in rushing rapids and then rested in calmer water for new battles. Mills stood along his banks; he worked diligently, he drove their wheels, he ground flour for many villages. Sawmills were built in his water; Roaring-Water sawed planks and boards night and day. Large rafts of logs swam on his back, boats sailed swiftly down his rushing waters. He grew and grew, and eventually he became a very large river, one of the largest in the world. I followed his riverbanks for months and years and saw how time after time big rivers and streams poured their water into his. As a result, Roaring-Water became increasingly powerful. I saw him carry great ships on his back and float through rich cities with untold thousands of people, who asked me: "Have you ever seen such a mighty river?" "No, I said, - but I have seen him as a small child; I have dammed his childhood spring with some pebbles, and the first ship he carried was my pea-pod boat."

"As Roaring-Water grew bigger, he became more useful but also more dangerous to humans. They built huge dams from shore to shore to tame his wicked temper, when he sometimes wanted to roar over the banks of his usual channel. One day in the spring the sun shone hot, and a lot of snow melted on the mountains and flowed in combative streams down into the river. This made Roaring-Water cavalier and wild. I saw him swell up high, throw himself over the dams, smash them down and flood many miles of a fertile and densely populated land."

"But there he met a crag which barred his way, and what did Roaring-Water do? He gathered his waters in a large lake in front of the crag and wrestled with the crag, but it would not yield its place. Finally, the lake rose higher and higher and reached the top of the crag and began to flow over it in the largest and most splendid waterfall ever seen. There was a roar and spray and mist in all the colours of the rainbow, and then Roaring-Water tumbled from a height of more than sixty meters, intent on seeking his destination, the great ocean far off in the distance. To get here, he still had a long way to go, and finally he grew tired of his own greatness and divided himself into many tributaries, which, shallow and sluggish, floated through a marshy land. Now Roaring-Water was old, he had lived life too fast, and therefore he became frail in his old age. The people regained power over his divided courses and dammed him here and there, at will. And when the time finally came for him to pass away into the sea, Roaring-Water, in many small channels, slipped quietly and wearily into the great eternal depths of oblivion."

"But I said to myself: Oh, dear heavens[1], now in Roaring-Water I have seen the depiction of a human life in its grandeur, its beauty, its usefulness, its pride, and its final fragility. And now I know that no power and no greatness on earth is eternal, but the great ocean awaits us all. Therefore, I believe we should seek, in humility, to use our greatness, our power, our purpose to work for Good!"[2]

"And now," said Richard, "the story of Roaring-Water is ended. I have come back wiser than when I went, but I cannot find my sister Rosa, so I am alone in the world with all my wisdom."

"No, Richard," said Rosa, "you are no longer alone, for now your sister's arms lie around your neck, and your sister's mouth kisses your mouth, and your sister's tears mix warmly with your tears. Now we should build a cottage here up on the meadow between Roaring-Water and Sighing-Stream, so that we will see them both and always remember their different destinies. Do you want that, Richard? Say that you will."

"Yes," said Richard, kissing Rosa's cheeks and hands. And so they built a cottage between Roaring-Water and Sighing-Stream and thereby, through images visible in Nature, always remembered the meaning and purpose of a good life.[3]

Eventually, Rosa and Richard became old, but the two brooks remained forever young; the streams were always the same small children, in whose clear mirror Rosa had previously nodded to the water-sprite's girl and where Richard had let the pea-pod boats swim with the current. Sighing-Stream was constantly murmuring just as quietly on summer evenings; Roaring-Water roared just as uncontrollably over sand and rocks. Though neither stream knew its eventual fate, Rosa and Richard knew theirs well enough, for they remembered their experiences as long as they lived.

A Raspberry Masquerade

"Ugh!" exclaimed Therese. "Oh my!" cried Aina.

"What now?" said Big Sister.

"A worm!" Therese shrieked. "On the raspberries!" cried Aina.

"Kill it," Lorenzo called out.

"Oh, so much fuss over a poor little worm[1]," said Big Sister scornfully.

"Yes, as we were cleaning the raspberries," said Therese, "it crawled out of the very biggest one."

"And if anyone had eaten that raspberry, they would have eaten the worm." added Aina.

"Well, what then?" said Lorenzo.

"Eaten a worm!" exclaimed Therese. "And bitten him to death," Aina grimaced.

"Of course," Lorenzo said laughing.

"Now it is crawling under the table," Therese shouted again.

"Shoo it away!" said Big Sister.

"Trample it to death," Lorenzo smiled.

But Therese took a raspberry leaf, gently swept the worm onto the leaf, and carried it out into the garden. Then Aina noticed that a sparrow was sitting on the fence, eager to scoop up the worm. Straightaway she took the leaf and the worm to the forest edge and hid them under the raspberry bushes, so that the malevolent sparrow could not find the worm's hiding place.

Well, what more is there to tell about a raspberry worm? Who would be bothered at all about such a tiny bug? Only the girls who lived in a dark red cottage surrounded by fresh, fragrant, rural splendour, far away in the tranquil forest amongst flowers and greenery!

Now it was close to noon, and so everyone ate raspberries and milk for lunch.

"Sprinkle just enough sugar, Lorenzo!" said Big Sister. But Lorenzo's plate looked like a snowdrift in the winter, with a little red under the snow.

Shortly after lunch, Big Sister said:

"Oh, now we have eaten all the raspberries and have nothing left to preserve for the winter. It would be nice to still have two full baskets of fresh berries; we could all clean them tonight, and tomorrow we could cook them in the big iron pot, and then we can eat waffles with raspberry jam!"

"Let's go to the forest and pick more," said Therese.

"Yes, we'll do that," said Aina. "You take the yellow basket; I'll take the green one."

"Don't get lost and come home safely by dusk!" said Big Sister.

"Say hi to the raspberry worm!" teased Lorenzo. "Next time I meet him, I'll have the honour of eating him."

So off went Aina and Therese into the forest. Oh, it was so beautiful there, so marvellous! Naturally, it was sometimes difficult to climb over fallen trees and they got caught by branches and scratched by juniper bushes and fought with the mosquitoes, but that didn't hold them back. The girls strode quickly on with their dresses tucked-in, and soon they were deep in the forest.

There were plenty of crowberries, blueberries and bunchberries[2] but few raspberries. The girls went farther, and finally they came ... no, it could not be true ... they came to a veritable jungle of raspberries. Once there had been a forest fire and now many raspberry bushes had grown up, as far as the eye could see. Each bush was weighed down by large, dark red, ripe raspberries.

Therese picked, Aina picked; Therese ate, Aina ate. After a while, their baskets were full.

"Now we should go home," said Aina.

"No, let's pick a few more!" said Therese. So, they put their baskets on the ground and picked up their aprons, and it was not long before the aprons were also full.

"Now we can go home," said Therese.

"Yes, let's go home," said Aina. Each girl took her basket in one hand and held up her apron with the other and they began to walk home.

But that was easier said than done. They had never been so far into the great forest. There were no paths or trails and soon the girls realized that they were lost. The worst thing was that the shadows of the trees grew longer in the evening sunshine, the birds began to fly home to their nests, and the dew started to fall. Finally, the sun went down behind the tops of the pines, and it became cool and gloomy in the great forest. The girls became anxious but kept going, hoping that the forest would soon end, and they'd see the smoke arising from their chimney.

After they had trekked a long while, it became dark. They came to a large clearing, overgrown with bushes, and when they surveyed as much as they could see in the darkness, they noticed that they had roamed around in a large circle and that they were back again among the many beautiful raspberry bushes where they had filled up their baskets and aprons earlier. Tired, they sat down on a rock and began to cry.

"I'm hungry," said Therese.

"Yes," said Aina. "Oh, if only we had two big sandwiches with some meat on them!"

As she said that, she felt something in her lap, and when she touched it, it was a large rye-bread sandwich with roasted chicken in it. At the same time, Therese said:

"This is odd, I have a sandwich in my hand."

"I also have one," said Aina. "Do you dare to eat it?"

"Of course I will," said Therese. "Oh, if only we had a tall glass of milk!'

As she said that, she felt a large glass of milk between her fingers. Shortly afterwards, Aina said:

"Therese! Therese! I have a glass of milk in my hand! This is really strange!"

However, as the girls were hungry, they ate and drank with a healthy appetite. When this was done, Aina yawned, stretched out her arms and said:

"Alas, if only we had a soft bed to sleep in!"

No sooner had she spoken, she felt a fine, soft bed next to her, and Therese noticed the same. The girls believed it was truly fantastic, but being so sleepy and tired, they thought no more about it and crawled into the beds, said their evening prayers, and pulled the covers over their heads. Soon they were both sound asleep.

When they awoke the sun was high in the sky. It was a lovely summer morning in the forest and the birds flew around merrily in the tree-tops and branches. In amazement, when they realized that they had slept in the forest among the raspberry bushes, the girls were lost for words. They looked at each other, they looked at their beds, which were covered with the finest linen, spread over soft leaves and maidenhair moss. Eventually, Therese said:

"Are you awake, Aina?"

"Yes," said Aina.

"But am I still dreaming?" said Therese.

"No," said Aina. "But surely a kind spirit lives here among these raspberry bushes. Oh, if only we had a cup of hot coffee and a good doughnut to dip into it!"

No sooner was this said, than next to them stood a small tray of silver with a gilt coffee-pot, two cups of real porcelain, a fine crystal sugar bowl, a silver cream-jug, and some good, warm wheat bread. The girls poured the extraordinary coffee into the cups, added sugar and cream, and tasted it. They had never drunk such good coffee.

"Now I would like to know who has given us all this," Therese said with a grateful expression.

"I have done all this, my dear little girls," said a voice from the bushes. In astonishment, the girls noticed a small friendly old man, in a white coat and red cap, hobbling out from the bushes, limping a little with his left foot. Therese and Aina were too amazed to say a word.

"Do not be afraid, little girls!" said the old man, grinning kindly at them, for he could not really laugh, his mouth was crooked. "Welcome to my domain! Have you slept well and eaten well and drunk well?" he asked.

"Yes, indeed we have," said both girls, "but tell us ..." and they wanted to ask who the old man was, but they did not dare.

"I will tell you who I am," 'said the old man. "I am the king of raspberries who rules over this whole realm of raspberry bushes, and I have lived here for thousands of years. But the Great Spirit, who rules over the forest and the sea and the sky, does not want me to be too proud of my royal power and my long life. Therefore, he has commanded that one day every hundred years I should be transformed into a little raspberry worm and live like such a weak and defenceless creature from sunrise until sunset. During this transformation, my survival depends on the life-chances of the little worm, so that a bird could eat me with its beak or a child could pick me with the berries and trample on my long life with their foot. Just yesterday was my day of transformation, and I was picked with the raspberries and was close to being trampled to death before you good-natured children saved me. All day until sunset I lay helpless in the grass, and when I was blown away from your table, I twisted one of my feet, and my mouth became crooked from terror. But when evening came and I regained my true form, I looked around for you to thank you and reward you. And then I found both of you here in my kingdom, and I received you as best I could, without frightening you too much. Now I will send one of my forest birds to show you the way home. Goodbye, dear children, thank you for your kindness. The raspberry king should show that he is not ungrateful."

The girls shook hands with the old man and thanked him, so happy that they had spared the little raspberry worm yesterday. They now wanted to go, but at that moment the old man turned once more, laughed mischievously with his crooked mouth, and said:

"Say hello to Lorenzo and say that when we meet next time, I will have the honour of eating him up."

"Oh, don't do that, dear raspberry king!" exclaimed both girls, greatly alarmed.

"Well, for your sake, let it be forgiven," replied the old man, "I'm not vindictive. Say hello to Lorenzo and tell him he will also receive a gift from me. Farewell!"

Now the girls took their berries and skipped, light of heart, as they followed the bird flying through the dense forest. In rather a short while, they saw the forest thin out and they marvelled that yesterday they had taken such long detours. And you can imagine what joy there was when the two girls arrived home. There, everyone had been waiting, everyone had been looking for them; Big Sister had not slept a wink, she was certain that the wolves had eaten up her dear little girls. But Lorenzo met them with a basket and shouted:

"Come and see, here's something an old man just brought here for you!"

When the girls opened the basket, they beheld two pairs of the most beautiful bracelets with dark red gemstones in the form of ripe raspberries, bearing the inscription: 'To Therese and Aina'. And next to them lay a diamond pin in the shape of a raspberry worm with the inscription: 'Lorenzo, never kill the defenceless!' Lorenzo was somewhat surprised: he probably understood the meaning, but still he thought that the old man had retaliated in the manner of gentlefolk. And the raspberry king had even thought of Big Sister, because when she went in to set the table for lunch, she found twelve large baskets with the biggest and sweetest raspberries ever picked in the forest, and no one knew how they got there, but everyone guessed. And then there was jam making and sugar and berry-boiling, the likes of which you've never seen, and if you want, we can go there and help them preserve ... It is likely that we'll get a turn to stir the pot, because they are probably still making jam there today.

Christmas with the Trolls

In the pretty little house at the corner of the street, it was bright and festive on Christmas Eve. Candles illuminated a large Christmas tree which was decorated with big stars, confectionery and apples. The three-branched candelabra burned brightly on the dining table and the children tried hard to keep still every time something creaked or rattled out in the hall. Eventually, Santa Claus[1] arrived and asked, as usual, if the children had been good. In unison, everyone answered yes.

"Is that so?" said Santa Claus. "If the children have been good, none of them should be left without a reward. But I want you to know that this year I have only half as many Christmas presents."

"Why is that?" asked the children.

"Let me tell you," said Santa Claus. "I have come all the way from the far north. There I knocked on the doors of numerous poor cottages and saw many small children who this year do not have a crust of bread to eat on Christmas Eve. That's why I gave half of all my gifts to them. Was that not the right thing to do?"

"Yes, yes, that was right, that was kind," the children shouted. Only Fredrik and Lotta kept quiet at first, because in the past Fredrik usually received twenty Christmas presents and Lotta often got thirty. Now they thought they would be destitute if they only got half as many.

"Was that the right thing to do?" asked Santa Claus for the second time.

Then Fredrik spoke up and grumpily answered: "Why is it such a rotten Christmas this year? The trolls have a better Christmas than you are giving us!"

Lotta began to whine, saying: "Will I get only fifteen Christmas presents? It would be a much, much better Christmas Eve with the trolls."

"Indeed," said Santa Claus, "if that's your attitude, I'll take you there right away." Then he seized Fredrik and Lotta, one in each hand, and dragged them away with him, even though they struggled with all their might.

Up and away, they flew quickly through the air. Before the children knew it, they were standing in the middle of a great forest amidst deep snow. It was terribly cold and the snow swirled about so that you could hardly see the tall pines which stood in the darkness all around, and close by in the forest the wolves could be heard howling. But Santa Claus - he was gone again straightaway. He did not have time to wait, because that night he still needed to visit so many children kinder than Fredrik and Lotta.

Both children started screaming and crying, but the more they yelled, the closer the wolves howled around them.

"Come, Lotta," said Fredrik. "We must try and find a cottage here in the forest."

"I think I see a little light over there among the trees," said Lotta. "Let's go there."

"It's not a light," said Fredrik. "It's just icicles glistening amongst the darkness of the trees."

"I think I see a large mountain in front of us," said Lotta. "Could it be Rastekais, where Sampo Lappelill[2] rode on the great wolf on Christmas Eve?"

"What are you saying!" replied Fredrik. "Rastekais is easily seven hundred kilometres from our home. Come, let's go up the mountain! There we can look around better."

That was more easily said than done. They struggled through the high snow drifts, over bushes and fallen trees, and after a good while climbed up onto the mountain. They noticed a small door, and something resembling light shone through the door. Fredrik and Lotta followed the light, and shortly afterwards they found to their great astonishment that it really was Rastekais and that they were with the trolls. But it was already too late to turn around, and besides, the wolves were so close that they were almost looking in through the door.

Terrified, Fredrik and Lotta stopped close by the door and saw in front of them a large hall, where the trolls celebrated Christmas as a pagan festival or Yule revel. There were probably many thousands of them, but all quite small, barely half a meter high, and all of them dressed in grey, wrinkled but very lively, just like those Sampo Lappelill had seen. They were not afraid of the dark, for instead of light, the trolls used frozen glowworms and rotten tree stumps that shone in the dark. But when some trolls wanted more light, they stroked the back of a large black cat so that she sparkled, and then many other trolls shouted: "No, stop it now, it's going to be too bright, we can't stand it!"

For there is something peculiar about all the trolls in the world, that they shun the light and become uncomfortable when someone sees them as they really are. So, the trolls' Yule party celebrated the short days and long nights at the end of the year. And the trolls believed, as they assumed every Yuletide (for one gladly believes what one most desires) that daylight was gone for good, replaced by endless night. So they danced merrily inside the mountain and rejoiced in their Yule revels.

It was clear that the trolls did not feel the cold at all. They feasted on ice cream in the cold winter night and blew on ice cubes so that they would not be too hot when put into their mouths. There were savoury treats of ferns and spider legs and a Christmas tree of ice crystals. One of the little trolls acted as a Yule goat.

The giant, cruel mountain king was not with the trolls this year. Ever since he had raged against the Inari vicarage[2], no one knew what had become of him. Many thought that he had fled to Spitsbergen to rule a pagan country, as far away as possible from Christian people. He had left his northern kingdom to Mundus, the king of evil and darkness, who sat there in the middle of the great hall. At his side sat the troll's queen, whose name was Caro, and both had long beards. They gave each other Yule presents just like ordinary people. King Mundus gave Queen Caro a pair of stilts so tall that when she stepped up onto them, she became the tallest and grandest woman in the whole world. Queen Caro gave King Mundus a pair of candlesnuffers[3] that were so enormous he could use them to quench all the lights of the world, and when he raised them up, all lights everywhere became extinguished. Some people would probably love to get such candlesnuffers as a Christmas present from the trolls.

Now King Mundus rose up from his throne and gave a rather extravagant speech to the assembled trolls. He proclaimed to them the demise of the realm of light, that the shadows of darkness would become eternal over all the land and that the trolls would rule the world. There was a powerful acclamation from all the trolls:

"Hooray! Hooray for our great King Mundus, for our beautiful Queen Caro, for the eternal dominion of evil and darkness! Hip, hip, hip, hooray!"

The king said: "Where is my chief scout, whom I sent up to the top of the mountain to check whether there is any gleam of light left in the world?"

The scout came forward and said: "Your Majesty, your power is great. It's all dark!"

After a while, the king said: "Where is my scout?" And the scout came into view.

"Your Majesty," he said, "I see far away on the horizon a very small light, like the twinkling of a star as it emerges from a black cloud."

And the king said, "Go back to the top of the mountain!"

Soon the king said: "Where is my scout?" And the scout returned.

"Your Majesty," he said, "the sky is overcast with heavy snow clouds, and I no longer see the little light."

The king said: "Go back to the mountain top!"

In a while, once again the king said: "Where is my scout?" On the scout's return, the king noticed that the scout was shaking and was completely blind.

The king said: "My faithful scout, why do you tremble? And how did you become blind?"

The scout said: "Your Majesty, the clouds have disappeared and a star, bigger and brighter than all the other stars, shines high up in the sky. Therefore, I am shaking and the sight of it has blinded me."

The king said: "What does this mean? Has not all light now vanished, and the reign of darkness become eternal?"

But all the trolls stood around in silence and trepidation and no one answered.

Finally, one of the crowd said: "Your Majesty, two human children stand here at the door. Let us ask them. Maybe they know more than we do."

The king said: "Call the children here." Fredrik and Lotta, feeling more than a little uncomfortable, were dragged to the king's throne. The queen saw their great fright and said to one of the trolls standing around the throne: "Let the poor youngsters refresh themselves with a little dragon's blood and some beetle scales, so that they can open their mouths!"

"Eat and drink! Eat and drink!" said a troll woman. But the children had no desire at all for such exotic treats.

The king said to the children: "Now you are here in my domain, and I have the power to transform you into crows or spiders. But I want to put a puzzle to you, and if you can explain this puzzle, I will let you go home without harm. Do you want to hazard a guess?"

"Yes," the children answered.

"Well then!" said the king. "What does it mean when a light rises in the middle of the darkest night of the year, when all light has vanished, and darkness and trolls rule the world? Far to the east, a star is visible, which shines brighter than all other stars and threatens to destroy my power. Tell me, children, what does the star mean?"

Lotta said: "That star, on Christmas Eve, rises above Bethlehem in Palestine and shines all over the world."

The king said: "Why does it shine like that?"

Fredrik said: "For tonight our Savior is born, and he is the light that enlightens the whole world. From tonight the sunlight begins to increase and the days become longer again."

The king began to tremble violently on his throne and asked again: "What is the name of the lord and king of light, who was born this night and who has come to save the world from the power of darkness?"

Both children said: "Jesus Christ, the Son of God."

Hardly was that said before the whole mountain began to shudder, quake and collapse. A gale blew through the great hall, overthrowing the king's throne. The star shone into the darkest chasms, and all the trolls were scattered like shadows and smoke, until there was nothing left but the Christmas tree of ice. It soon began to glisten and melt, and high up in the air angelic voices were heard, ringing like harps. The children covered their faces with their hands and did not dare to look up. They fell into a deep, exhausted sleep and they no longer knew what was happening on the mountain.

When they awoke, they were both at home in their own beds. The fire was burning in the tiled corner stove, and old Kajsa, who always used to wake them, stood beside their beds, and said to them: "Hurry up, time to get ready for church!"

Fredrik and Lotta sat up and looked in amazement at Kajsa, as if she might be just a half-meter tall and had a beard and wanted to offer them dragon's blood and beetle scales. But instead, they noticed that the coffee table was already prepared with fresh Christmas buns and on Christmas morning all the children got coffee as a special treat. Outside, bells rang, and a throng of people made their way to the church. Lights were seen in all the windows, but those in the church shone the brightest.

Fredrik and Lotta looked at each other and did not dare tell Kajsa that they had been to the trolls' Yule revels. Maybe she would not have believed them; she would have laughed and said that they had slept all night in their beds. You and I think we know what happened, but we cannot really appreciate what it was like to be there. One thing I do know and that is that, sooner or later, discontented children always meet up with the trolls. There they get ice cubes, dragon blood and beetle scales instead of the good gifts they disdained to receive at home.

Fredrik and Lotta could never forget the trolls' Yule. Not only had they missed out on all the Christmas presents, but they also felt so ashamed of themselves that they did not dare venture to lift up their eyes in church on Christmas morning. There it was bright and beautiful, and the star of Bethlehem had come down and lit all the candles and was reflected in the gleaming eyes of all the good children. Fredrik and Lotta were aware of this, still did not dare to look up, but resolved to become good children. Have they kept their promise? I do not know, but I like to think so. When you meet them, you can ask them yourself.

The Sea King's Gift

There was once a fisherman named Laxmatte who lived by the seaside with Laxmaja, his wife. In the winter they lived in a small cottage on the mainland shore but in the spring they migrated to an isle of red rock far out to sea. They lived there all summer, until autumn came, in an even smaller hut, which had a wooden latch instead of a lock, a grey stone stove, a flagpole, and a weathervane on the roof.

The isle was called Ahtola and was no larger than the market square in town. A small rowan and four alder bushes grew in the rock's crevices. Goodness knows how they got there - maybe with the autumn storms. In addition to the bushes, there were some tussocks of velvety grass, one or two reed beds, and a few flowering plants; some with yellow flowers, called tansy, red-flowered fireweed and ones with a beautiful white flower, called arctic starflower. But the rarity on the isle was three clumps of chives, which Laxmaja had purposely planted in a gulley, with a stone wall on the north side and sun on the south. It was not much, but it was enough for Laxmaja's herb garden.

They say all good things come in threes, and that's why Laxmatte and Laxmaja fished for salmon in the spring, baltic herring in the summer and whitefish in the autumn. If the weather was fine and the wind was favourable, they sailed into town on Saturday, sold the fresh fish and went to church on Sunday. But often they were marooned on Ahtola isle for several weeks in a row and saw nothing but their little golden-brown mutt (proudly named Prince), the grass, bushes and flowers, the seagulls and fish, the stormy sky and the pale blue waves. For the isle lay at the outermost edge of the archipelago, and there was no green island or human habitation for miles around, only here and there an isle of the same red rock as Ahtola, showered with the foam of the waves day and night.

Laxmatte and Laxmaja were modest and industrious people, contented and happy to live on their own with Prince in their simple hut. They fancied themselves rich when, having salted enough firkins[1] of fish to tide themselves over the winter, they had a little left over to trade for tobacco for Laxmatte 's pipe and a few pounds of coffee for Laxmaja, mixed with roasted barley and chicory to 'improve' the taste. In addition, they had butter, bread, fish, a barrel of small-beer[2] and a cooler for sour milk. What more did they need?

Now everything would have been fine if Laxmaja had not nursed a secret desire that gave her no peace. She pondered year in and year out how she could become rich enough to finally afford a cow.

"What are you going to do with a cow?" asked Laxmatte. "How would we get her out here to the isle - she couldn't swim that far, and she wouldn't fit in our boat. And if we got her out here, then we would have nothing to feed her."

"We have four alder bushes and sixteen tussocks of grass," said Laxmaja.

"Well, why not?" laughed Laxmatte. "There are also three clumps of chives. You can feed her on chives."

"All cows like salted herring," said Laxmaja. "Prince also likes fish."

"I find that hard to believe!" said Laxmatte. "No, thank you, but it would be an expensive cow if we fed her on salted herring. It works for Prince, who fights with the seagulls for the leftovers when we gut the herring. Put the cow out of your mind, woman, everything's fine as it is!"

Laxmaja sighed. She knew that Laxmatte was right, but she could not forget about the cow. The old sour milk no longer tasted like cream in the coffee, and Laxmaja thought of sweet cream and bowls of fresh yogurt as the greatest bliss imaginable.

One day, while the man and woman were gutting herring by the shore, they heard Prince barking, and a fine painted sloop with three young men in white sailor's caps appeared, steering for the isle. The sailors, students on a long-distance pleasure cruise, sought land in order to get fresh supplies.

"Row out here with a pan of fresh yogurt, dear lady!" they shouted.

"Oh, if only I had some!" sighed Laxmaja.

"May we have a jug of fresh whole milk?" the students said.

"Oh, if only I had some!" groaned Laxmaja.

"What? You don't have a cow?"

Laxmaja remained silent. It upset her too much to answer such a delicate question.

"We do not have a cow," replied Laxmatte, "but if you'd like some good smoked herring, they will be ready in a couple of hours."

"We'll wait for the buckling[3]", the students said, and without ceremony settled down on the rocks with their cigars and pipes, while fifty silver-white herrings, threaded on skewers, went in the smoke oven.

"What is the name of this pebble in the sea?" asked one of them.

"Ahtola," Laxmatte replied.

"Well, you should need for nothing then, when you live on the sea-king's estate!"

Laxmatte did not understand. He had never heard of or read the Kalevala[4] and knew nothing about the legendary sea gods. But the students happily enlightened him.

"In our Finnish folklore," they explained, "Ahti is a mighty king, who lives in his castle, Ahtola, on a rock in the deep sea surrounded by all sorts of precious treasures. He rules over all the fish and other sea creatures; he has the most splendid cows and the fastest horses, which graze the seagrass on the seabed. Anyone who gets on well with Ahti will soon become a rich man; however, one must be very careful not to annoy him in the least. For Ahti can be very fickle and crabby. He can be annoyed by a small rock thrown into the water, and then he takes his gifts back and raises up the sea into a storm and drags the sailor down into the depths. Ahti also has the most beautiful handmaidens, who care for his queen, Wellamos; they hold up and comb her long hair and listen in the reeds, when one plays music for them…"

"Oh, the Necken[5]!" said Laxmatte. "Have you gentlemen seen him?"

"It is as good as if we had seen these spirits ourselves," the students said. "It is printed in books, and everything printed must be true."

"You don't say," replied Laxmatte, a little scornfully. "In that case, we should have had beautiful weather yesterday, because it said in the almanac that it would be clear, but in fact it was windy and pouring with rain, as if the heavens had opened."

"Well look, that comes about because the almanac printer takes the freedom to tell a fib, in jest, and when this falsehood is printed, the false news is believed to be true," the students said.

Laxmatte shook his head. Soon, the buckling was done, the students ate enough for six and treated Prince to a cold steak, which they had with them in the sloop. Prince sat up with joy on his hind legs and purred like a cat. When all was done, the students gave Laxmatte a shiny silver Finnish mark and let him fill his pipe with good Gefle tobacco, whereupon Laxmatte stuffed the pipe until it cracked. Then the gentlemen gave thanks for the banquet and went on their way, much missed by Prince, who sat on the shore, and with a melancholy gaze, followed the white patch of sail as it faded away on the distant blue sea.

Laxmaja had not said a word, but her thoughts were racing. She had good ears and had memorized the story of Ahti to the letter. 'Well, that would be amazing,' she thought to herself, 'to get one of those enchanted cows! How wonderful it would be to milk such a marvellous cow, morning and evening, and not have any concerns about her feed, but only worry about finding enough space in the pantry to store all the jugs of fresh milk and bowls of yogurt! But I will probably never have such good fortune in this life.'

"What are you thinking about?" asked Laxmatte.

"Oh nothing," said the woman. But quietly she thought of some old magic spells, those she had heard in her childhood from a lame old man, reputed to conjure up good luck when fishing. 'What if I were to try that?' she thought.

Now it was a Saturday, and on Saturday evening, Laxmatte did not usually put out his herring nets, for their religious teaching forbade working on Sunday, when the laden nets would need to be brought in. But as the evening wore on, Laxmaja said, "Tonight we should put our nets out."

"No," said Laxmatte, "No good will come from fishing on Sunday."

"Last night it was stormy, and we got so few fish," said Laxmaja. "Tonight, the sea is as smooth as a mirror, and as the wind dies down, the herring moves inshore."

"But there is a storm cloud in the northwestern sky," said Laxmatte, "and Prince was eating grass this evening."

"I hope he hasn't eaten my chives?" asked Laxmaja.

"No, but it means there will be rough weather tomorrow at sunrise," said Laxmatte.

"Now listen," said Laxmaja; "we lay out a single net leeward of the reef, and then we will catch enough to fill that firkin we have open. It shouldn't stand there long without the lid locked down."

Laxmatte let himself be persuaded, and they rowed out with the nets. Out on the open sea, Laxmaja began to croon the old magic spell, changing the words according to her heart's desire:

"Ahti with the flowing beard,
Ahti of the deep sea,
You have many fine treasures,
The fish of the sea are yours,
Pearls without equal
Gather in your kingdom,
The beautiful fat cows of the sea,
Graze on your verdant meadows ..."

"What is that you're crooning?" asked Laxmatte.

"It's just an old song that came to mind," Laxmaja replied, and then she raised her voice and continued to sing:

"King of the vast waters,
I'm not asking for golden treasure,
I'm not asking for pearl jewellery,

Nor is silver my fancy.

One is one and two is two:

King of the sea, give me a cow,

And as reward I will give you

The sun's gold and the moon's silver…"

"That's a silly song," said Laxmatte. "Why would one ask for anything other than fish from the sea king? And I feel it is not appropriate to sing such things on the evening before Sunday."

Laxmaja pretended not to hear him and continued singing in the same low voice, all the while that they were out on the open sea. Laxmatte no longer listened, for as he sat rowing the heavy boat, he thought of his cracked clay pipe and the fine Gefle tobacco. Eventually, they got back to their isle and soon afterwards retired to bed.

Laxmatte and Laxmaja lay in their bed but neither of them fell asleep; one regretted having to work on Sunday, the other thought of Ahti's cows. When it grew past midnight, Laxmatte sat up in bed and said to Laxmaja: "Do you hear anything?"

"No," said Laxmaja.

"I think the weathervane on the roof is creaking," said Laxmatte. "We're getting a storm."

"Ah, you're imagining it," said Laxmaja.

Laxmatte lay down, but after a while he sat up again. "Now the weathervane is squeaking," he said.

"Go back to sleep; you're dreaming," said Laxmaja. And Laxmatte tried to sleep.

But the third time, he jumped out of bed. "No, now the weathervane is shrieking, as if it's on fire! Now we're getting a storm and have to go out to salvage the nets". Both now arose, and the summer night was as dark as October, and the weathervane whistled, and the storm howled from all directions. When they got outdoors, the great sea heaved like drifting snow all around them in the night, and the foam splashed high above the roof of the fisherman's hut. Laxmatte couldn't remember ever having experienced such a night. Pushing out the boat and going to sea to salvage the nets was out of the question. In astonishment, Laxmatte and Laxmaja stood at the doorstep and had to hold on to the doorpost while the salt spray splashed their faces.

"Did I not say that fishing on a Sunday is never a good idea?" said Laxmatte bitterly, and Laxmaja just stood there, so aghast and terrified that she did not even think of Ahti's cows. When they saw nothing could be done, they went back inside. After their night vigil, their eyes became heavy, and they fell soundly asleep despite the stormy sea rushing in anger around their lonely isle. When Laxmatte and Laxmaja awoke, the sun was already high in the sky and the tempest had ceased, while the sea-swell surged in silver breakers, glistening in the sunshine, against the red rock.

"Oh no, what is this?" cried Laxmaja, as she looked out the door.

"It looks like a big bull seal," said Laxmatte.

"As I live and breathe, if it isn't a cow!" exclaimed Laxmaja.

And it was a cow, a splendid red cow of the best breed, plump and plush, as if she had eaten spinach all her days. She walked calmly around the shore but did not even touch the poor turf, as if she despised such a meagre diet.

Laxmatte could not believe his eyes. But it was a cow, in full working order, which soon became apparent when the old woman began to milk her and filled all their vessels, right down to the boat bailer, with the sweetest morning milk. Laxmatte's mind wrestled in vain to understand how she got there and then he went out to look for his lost nets. It was not long before he found them thrown up by the waves onto the shore, completely full of fine shimmering herring.

"It's all well and good that we have a cow," said Laxmatte, as he gutted the herring. "But with what shall we feed her?"

"We shall manage somehow," said Laxmaja.

The cow found its own solution. She waded out into the water and ate the seagrass which grew in large banks by the shore; thus she always kept herself in the best condition. Everyone except Prince thought she was a decent cow. Prince barked at her; he now had a rival.

From that day on, there was an abundance of milk cans and pans of yoghurt on the red isle. All the nets were constantly full of fish. Laxmatte and Laxmaja grew fat from luxurious living and became richer every day, for Laxmaja earned well from selling butter while Laxmatte took on two assistants and started fishing in a big way. For him the sea became a large fish farm from which he hauled up as much as he could handle. And the cow continued to take care of herself. In the autumn, when Laxmatte and Laxmaja moved back to the mainland, the cow went into the sea, and in the spring, when they returned, she stood again on the isle.

"We need a better cabin," said Laxmaja the second summer. "The old one is now far too small for us and the deckhands."

"Yes," said Laxmatte. And soon he built a magnificent cottage on the isle with a proper lock and a shed for curing fish and took on two more deckhands and fished so prodigiously that he sent many barrels of salmon, herring and whitefish to Russia and Sweden.

"I am wearing myself out with people's demands," said Laxmaja. "It would be a good idea if I got a milkmaid to help me."

"Get yourself one," said Laxmatte. And so they hired a milkmaid.

But then Laxmaja said: "We have far too little milk to feed people and sell at market. Now I have a maid, she could take care of three cows as easily as one."

"Then you should go out and sing another magic song," said Laxmatte, a little scornfully.

This annoyed Laxmaja. Nevertheless, one Sunday night she rowed out on the open sea, singing as before:

"Ahti with the flowing beard,

Ahti in the deep waters,

You have a thousand cows grazing,

Give me three of them!"

The next morning, three cows stood on the isle instead of one, and they all ate the seagrass and took care of themselves like the first.

"Are you satisfied now?" said Laxmatte to his wife.

"Of course I would be happy," said Laxmaja, "if only I had two more maids for the big household and also got some better clothes. Have you not heard that I'm now called Madam?"

"Well, alright," said Laxmatte. Laxmaja got several maids and smart ladies' outfits.

"Everything could be so good now," she said, "if we just made a few improvements for the summer. You should build us a two-story house and bring soil there so that we might construct a garden. There you could build a small gazebo, that I might look out over the sea, and then we could have a fiddler to play a bass violin for us in the evenings; and then we should have our own little steamboat to go to church with when it was windy."

"Is that all?" said Laxmatte. And he put together all his wife wished for. The Ahtola isle became so grand, and Laxmaja became so distinguished, that all the sea's cod and herring gaped in amazement. Prince was fed on veal roast and waffles with cream and eventually became as round as a sprat barrel.

"Are you happy now?" asked Laxmatte

"Of course I'd be satisfied," said Laxmaja, "if only I had thirty cows. That's a herd worthy of our household.

"Use your magic," said Laxmatte.

Laxmaja went out in her new steamboat and sang for the sea king. The next morning, thirty beautiful cows stood on the shore, and they all took care of themselves.

"You know, husband," said Laxmaja, "it's altogether too crowded here on such a small, wretched isle, and where can I find enough room for so many cows?"

"I know of no other solution, said Laxmatte, "than that you pump out the sea."

'What are you saying? Who can pump out the sea?"

"Try with your new steamboat, it has a pump."

Laxmaja well understood that the man was being ridiculous but could not stop thinking about it. 'I cannot pump out the sea,' she thought. 'But maybe I could fill it in somewhat if I build a big breakwater against the sea. I can lay down stones and sand here, and we will make our rocky isle twice as big.'

Laxmaja loaded her new steamboat with rocks at the mainland and came back over the open sea. The fiddler accompanied her and played so beautifully on his bass violin, that Ahti and Wellamo and all the maidens of the sea rose to the surface to listen to the recital.

"What is it that glitters so brilliantly amongst the waves?" Laxmaja asked.

"It is the sea foam that glistens in the sunshine," the fiddler replied.

"Heave out the rocks!" said Laxmaja.

The people in the steamboat began to jettison the rocks to the right and left of the foam. Splash, plop, a rock struck the nose of Wellamo's favourite handmaiden. Another scratched the cheek of the sea queen herself. A third rock plummeted close to Ahti's head and tore away half of the sea king's beard. There was a commotion in the sea, and the waves roiled over each other as if in a boiling cauldron.

"Where did this bad weather come from?" said Laxmaja. But before she finished speaking, the sea yawned wide like the gape of a giant pike and swallowed the whole steamboat. Laxmaja sank like a rock to the bottom, but struggling with her hands and feet, she got back up to the surface, where she grabbed the fiddler's bass violin and kept afloat on that. She came next to Ahti's terrifying head and saw he had only half a beard.

"Why did you throw rocks at me?" roared the sea king.

"Ah, merciful lord," wheedled Laxmaja, "it was a mistake. Apply bear grease[6] to your beard, and it will soon grow back."

"Lady, have I not given you everything you asked for and more?"

"Yes, of course, gracious lord. Many thanks for the cows! They milk wonderfully."

'Well then, where are the sun's gold and the moon's silver that you promised me?"

"Ah, gracious lord, why they have shone on the sea every day and night, when it has not been overcast," Laxmaja answered cunningly.

"I'll teach you!" cried the sea-king and gave the bass violin such a blast that it flew, together with the old woman, like a rocket towards the isle. There stood Prince, as hungry as in the past, gnawing on a crow's bone. Laxmatte sat alone in his threadbare grey jacket on the stairs up to the old poor hut and repaired a net.

"Look at you, woman!" he said. "Where have you come from, flying at such a speed, and how are you so wet?"

Laxmaja looked around in astonishment and said: "Where is our two-story house?"

'What house?" said Laxmatte.

"Our big house and the garden and the deckhands and the milkmaids and the thirty beautiful cows and the steamboat and everything else?"

"Now you're talking out of your nightcap, woman," said Laxmatte. "The students have so confused your mind that you sang crazy songs last night out on the sea, and you couldn't sleep until dawn. There was a storm last night, but it's over now, and I did not bother to wake you, but rowed out alone to gather in the nets."

"But I've seen Ahti," said Laxmaja.

"You've been lying in your bed dreaming nothing but craziness, woman, and then you went sleepwalking out into the water."

"But there's the bass violin," said Laxmaja.

"Beautiful bass violin! It's just an old log. No, dear lady, in future we should be careful not to go fishing on Sunday. It never brings good fortune."

Bullerbasius

Lasse was six years old and a little shorter than his sister Hilda, who was ten years old and thought of herself as a mother to Lasse. Both bickered all day and hardly realized how much they cared for each other. But they noticed it when they were apart. When Hilda was away at school, Lasse became terribly sad and was naughty all day. And when Lasse travelled with his father to the Forsa factory, Hilda was at a loss all week and did not know what to do while Lasse was gone.

Hilda undertook to keep a journal of Lasse's mischief, with the laudable intention of reading this marvellous account to him at the appropriate opportunity. She reckoned that this rebuke would serve as a warning to Lasse, so that he would be really ashamed of his stupidity.

One cloudy day before Christmas, when Hilda was off from school and Lasse had been more than usually mischievous, Hilda called to him: "Lasse, come here!"

Lasse was sitting in a corner, trying to reattach a hind leg of his wooden horse, which he had broken when the horse wouldn't gallop as fast as he wished. He was in a bad mood and pretended not to hear.

"Come here, and I will read something to you," said Hilda, somewhat slyly, for she had just taken out the remarkable diary.

Lasse came to her. Like all of us, he enjoyed stories and thought that perhaps Hilda wanted to read to him about the troll Lunkentus or the ignoble Bluebeard.

"Sit down on the stool and be good and quiet, and you will hear the exploits and adventures of the robber chief Bullerbasíus Rummelfelt."

Lasse sat down meekly, and Hilda began her prologue:

"There was once a robber chief, named Bullerbasius and so on. He had a fairy godmother, and after Bullerbasius had made so much trouble in the world, his godmother created a book, in which she wrote down what he had done. She then decided to have that book published in Stockholm, so that all the people would know how wicked and unwise Bullerbasius had been. Now, you see, I have borrowed the godmother's book, before it is sent to Stockholm to be printed, and now you will hear everything that Bullerbasius has to be ashamed of."

Lasse pricked up his ears. He had never heard of such a robber chief.

Hilda kept a straight face and read from the diary:

"January 1st. Bullerbasius began the year by kicking his bed apart, and when he got up, he put one of his socks in the washbasin to see if it floated on the water. Then Mamma came in - for he had a mamma - and gave him a slap with the wet sock. Was that not well deserved?"

Lasse looked surprised and said nothing.

"January 6th. The grey cat lay on the carpet in front of the tiled corner-stove. Bullerbasius picked up the cat, put her in the tiled stove and closed the doors. There had not been a fire since yesterday, but there were still embers, and the cat started to make a horrendous howling. Pappa came in - because Bullerbasius also had a pappa - freed the cat and ordered Bullerbasius to take a glowing coal in his hand. Bullerbasius wanted to run away, but Pappa put a coal in his hand and let him burn himself a little. Then Bullerbasius cried out ..."

"Oh no, I did not cry out," said Lasse.

"Here it says that Bullerbasius cried out."

"February 2nd. The boys were on the toboggan run, and Bullerbasius was with them. Then Bullerbasius decided to bury his hat in the snow, so that it would not be found until springtime when the snowdrifts melted. But later his left ear got frostbitten, which served as a warning."

"Because I could not find the hat!"

"Keep listening! February 20th. Mamma had eggs in a basket, which was kept in the drawing room, which no one used during the winter, and where it stayed cool enough. Bullerbasius found the basket under the drawing room sofa and had fun knocking one egg against another, so that they cracked and ran out all over the fine green fabric that covered the sofa. For that amusement, Bullerbasius was detained in the pantry, but there he found a jar of jam and emptied the jar with his fingers. For that affair, he was locked up again in his Pappa's room, and there he kept quiet."

Lasse laughed, a little embarrassed.

"Yes, wasn't that a foolish robber? continued Hilda. "Now listen on."

"March 7th. Bullerbasius also had a sister ..."

"Her name was Hilda," Lasse chimed in.

"I believe her name was Melusina. She had an extremely beautiful and lovable doll that had real hair and perfect eyes and her name was Ellen. When Melusina was at school, Bullerbasius took Ellen and poked out one of her eyes to see what was inside. Then he hung Ellen on the fireplace damper by her hair, so that she could swing. When Melusina came home and saw poor Ellen, she began to cry."

Lasse blushed and stamped the heels of his boots against the floor.

Hilda continued:

"Then Bullerbasius also began to cry, asked his sister for forgiveness and was not content until Pappa got the doctor to repair Ellen's eye. Was that good, that he repented?"

"Yes, but good also that Ellen got well again," said Lasse.

"Just a pity that Bullerbasius had such a short memory. For one week later, on March 14th, Bullerbasius was going out skiing and had carelessly lost his woollen gloves. Then he found Mamma's fine white French gloves, put them on his paws and went out into the snowdrifts. When he got home, all four of his fingers were sticking out of one glove, and the other glove was lost in the snow. Was that nice?"

"My hands were cold."

"Mamma scolded him, but Bullerbasius didn't get any wiser. On April 1st, he wanted to scare the maid, old Kajsa. He placed two chairs on top of each other inside the hall door and put a stool on top and on the stool a flowerpot. Judge Agander came in through the door, instead of Kajsa, and he almost died with fright when the chairs fell and the flowerpot broke. Then Bullerbasius was punished again."

"On April 20th, Bullerbasius wanted to try his skill as an archer and shot an arrow in through the kitchen window. Got away with a warning."

"On May 2nd, he pulled tail-feathers off the rooster and was punished with an hour's detention in the hen house. On May 4th he rowed out on the brook in a dough trough[1], overturned the trough and came home drenched. On the 18th, he filled his hat with stones and sank it in the lake while using it as a bucket. On May 22nd, Mamma had sown peas in the morning, and in the evening Bullerbasius dug up the pea-bed to see if the peas had grown. He was chastised and told not to be so silly next time."

"On May 23rd he broke a teacup, then ground it up with a pestle and mortar and wanted to trick Kajsa into believing that it was sugar."

"On Midsummer's Day, Bullerbasius did so many stupid things that it is impossible to list them ..."

"Ah no," said Lasse. "I only tore two holes in my sweater: one big and one small."

"Listen on," continued Hilda. "On July 6th he dug a hole in the garden and laid Pappa's signet ring, Mamma's thimble, six pinecones and a frog in the pit. Then he filled the pit with sand. It was supposed to be a secret hoard. Throughout the house, a fruitless search was made for the signet ring and the thimble, until suspicious enquiries were directed at Bullerbasius. Finally, he confessed that he had buried the treasure and was sent to bed without any supper. Was that fair?"

"But I meant no harm," said Lasse.

"Fie! He still didn't regret the disruption that his pleas of ignorance caused. Bullerbasius still had a guilty conscience because he stayed away at the neighbouring farm all the next day. So, his punishment was just. On July 28th, he walked on stilts, stumbled, and fell straight into the middle of the glass cucumber-frame. On July 30th, he went down to the shore without permission, pushed the boat out and started to row. But the wind blew hard, and our good man drifted out to sea. Then he started shouting for help."

"I would have been able to row, but the oars were too long."

"And the rower was too short. Then Matts rowed out with the big boat and brought the fellow back to shore. Bullerbasius's fright was punishment enough. The next day he rode on the bell-cow[2], fell off and knocked a hole in his head."

"I have ridden many horses!"

"That's as maybe," continued Hilda. "On August 11th, Bullerbasius also wanted to ride on the stud ram Pelle. But Pelle felt insulted and lowered his horns. Bullerbasius took flight and Pelle followed. Finally, they confronted each other by the stable wall, and had Kajsa not happened to come out with the milk pail from the cowshed, there would have been a great disaster."

"I beat him, yes, I beat him so ..."

"It says here that, in his mind, Bullerbasius struck Pelle, but in reality, he shouted: 'sweet Kajsa, come and help me!'"

"Yeah, when my stick broke!"

"Keep listening. On August 19th, Bullerbasius got sick from eating half-ripe gooseberries. On August 22nd he brought down the mill's weathervane. On the 29th he made Ellen (the doll) go for a swim in the brook. On the 30th he fell into the brook himself. On September 4th, Bullerbasius drew schoolmaster Långman's portrait with charcoal on the newly whitewashed tiled stove in the kitchen. For that he was confined to his room."

"Yes, but I climbed out the window," objected Lasse.

"And then Bullerbasius was detained in the attic, from where he refrained from stepping out of the window. On September 18th, everyone went picking lingonberries in the forest, and Bullerbasius chased after a squirrel and fell into a swamp. There he lost one of his boots and ruined his new trousers. On the 20th he was digging up potatoes and cut his leg with the hoe. On the 24th he fell out of the rowan tree."

"On October 4th, he ran through all the rooms with his dirty boots, looking for his hat, and found it in the firewood bin, where he had hidden it, full of sand. On the 8th he came home with his arms full of turnips, given to him by a boy who unfortunately had stolen them.

"I didn't know that."

"No, he had not known that, and therefore he was not punished. But he had to carry the turnips back himself to the Nygård's farm, where they had been stolen from. On the 16th he took a sip from a bottle of aniline oil and became quite ill. On the 17th he was such a bold boy again that he drove nails through the holes in his mother's brass colander. The sieve was ruined, and so as not to repeat the same foolish prank, our good man undertook on the 18th to wedge a plug in the spout of the coffee pot. On the 29th, while Kajsa was spinning, he amused himself by setting fire to her flax bundle, for which pleasure he was punished again. On November 3rd, he sneaked down to the skating pond without permission, knocked over another boy, who fell in through the thin ice, and then pulled him out. For this, Bullerbasius was first given detention and then a cake."

"I was praised too," Lasse objected proudly.

"You did not do a good deed to deserve cakes and praise," said Hilda. "It was worse on December 4th. Then Bullerbasius got into a quarrel with the Nygård boys about a great rarity which they found in the stable - a dead rat. Bullerbasius hit Calle Nygård with his cane and gave him a big bruise over the eye, even though Calle Nygård was smaller than he was. For this, Bullerbasius was required to ask Calle for forgiveness, but he did not want to."

"It was Calle who hit me first," said Lasse.

"Yes, but Calle was only four years old, and Bullerbasius was six. For shame, to beat such a little boy! And when Bullerbasius refused to ask forgiveness, he got a caning from Pappa. That was the first time in the whole year. Bullerbasius was compelled to ask for forgiveness, but then came the worst. He pleaded with his mouth, but not with his heart. A few days later, when the boys were snowballing, Bullerbasius moulded a very hard snowball and threw it at Calle. The ball hit Calle on the cheek, and his cheek swelled up. What do you call that?"

Lasse was silent.

"It is called revenge, and revenge is, next to ingratitude and falsehood, the ugliest thing that exists in a person's heart. A vindictive man is the enemy of God, and all the angels in heaven weep over him. How can such a person's spirit ever find true happiness and peace?"

Lasse clenched his teeth and made a strange grimace to hold back his tears. After a while he got up from the stool and walked away without saying a word.

Hilda knew her dear brother, pretended not to notice the grimace, and did not ask him to stay. In half an hour Lasse returned, beaming with pleasure.

"Where have you been?" asked Hilda.

"It was like this," said Lasse, a little embarrassed, "that ... you remember my toboggan, which I got as a present last Christmas? I called it Moppe, and there was never a better toboggan than Moppe."

"Yes," said Hilda, "I remember that you like Moppe more than Matts likes our best horse, and you always brag that no one has such a good sled."

"Now I have given Moppe to Calle Nygård. He was so happy; you can't imagine how awfully glad he was!

"And what about you then, Lasse? Aren't you happy too?"

"Yes, you know, Hilda, I've been so sorry for the dead rat, and I've been so wicked ever since, and it's so tiresome ... and when you told me about how the angels of God wept, I wanted to weep with them … and so I went to Calle, you see ... and now it's all good again, now I'm so terribly happy, you know, that now it's going to be really fun this Christmas."

Hilda hugged Lasse, kissed him and danced seven laps around the room with him.

"You know what?" she said. "Now when the fairy godmother of Bullerbasius sends her diary to be printed in Stockholm, we will ask her to highlight the dead rat. That story was both the dumbest and the smartest thing Bullerbasius did the whole year."

"Ask her to talk about the sister Melusina too! Because, you see, if Melusina had not existed, Bullerbasius would have been a real rascal."

"Oh, maybe it won't turn out so badly for Bullerbasius! He is sometimes maligned, but God has given him an honest heart; probably it will make a man of him."

And so, that was the story of the robber chief.

The Water Nymph's Silver Bowl

There was once a girl named Lisalill. Her father and mother were dead, and she lived with her blind grandfather in a dilapidated cabin on an island called Ängsholmen[1]. Who knows what they lived on during the long winter? Certainly, Grandpa was paid to mend other fishermen's nets and Lisalill made birch-twig brushes, which she sold in the town, but that income did not go far. Yet they scraped by without complaining.

They had a small wooden skiff and four nets, and they went fishing with them in the summer. And when the strawberries began to ripen on the forest slopes, the old man sat with his fishing rod in the boat, while Lisalill went up to the forest to pick berries. One day with the sun was blazing hot, they rowed to the outer shore of Elgö island, towards the open sea. Grandfather became thirsty.

"Lisalill" he said, "take the jug and fetch me some water from a spring; I cannot drink the sea water, it's too salty."

"I will get that for you," said Lisalill, who was always nimble and obedient, and so she took the jug and jumped ashore. It was a rather wild and rugged area, nothing but rocks and dark forest. Lisalill ran up hill and down dale until she became completely flushed with the heat and exertion, but found no source, for there was a summer drought and all the water had dried up. Finally, she became tired and slowed her pace. As she walked under the dark pines, she began to imagine strange, new thoughts. She thought that the tall trees looked down on her rather oddly, and she felt so lonely, all alone in the world. Then something rustled in the branches above her, and she heard a squeaky voice, which said to her:

"Why do you walk all alone, Lisalill? Where is your sweetheart?"

Lisalill looked up and saw nothing but a hazelhen[2] sitting on the swaying bough of an old birch. She became frightened and began to run, but quickly she stumbled over a tree stump and with a crash, there lay her clay jug in twenty pieces. Goodbye, pitcher!

Well, that was that. Now grandfather was waiting alone in the boat, and what would Lisalill use to fetch water to quench his thirst? Lisalill sat down on a tree stump and began to cry. Then she heard another voice, cooing between the trees:

"Why do you walk all alone, Lisalill? Where is your sweetheart?"

Lisalill looked around but noticed only a squirrel, who was looking furtively through the branches of a leafy spruce. This annoyed her. What business was it of the squirrel if she walked alone in the woods? So, she turned her back on it and went in a different direction. But she had not gone far before she heard the same question for the third time:

"Why do you walk all alone, Lisalill? Where is your sweetheart?"

Now it was a beautiful, unfamiliar bird with gold on its wings, flying high in the blue sky.

"What kind of stupid talk is that?" said Lisalill. "Grandpa is sitting in the skiff waiting for water, and I have broken our only jug."

"Yes, but where is your sweetheart?" asked the golden bird from on high in the blue sky.

"Well, what a foolish bird!" said Lisalill. "Does it not know that I love my Grandpa more than anyone else on earth? And yet it asks about my sweetheart."

Lisalill thought such questions were quite impolite, and so she went back towards the seashore to seek out her grandfather. But was she left in peace? Not a chance! Now all of the trees, bushes and rocks began to come to life all around her. The tree-stumps found a voice, the lingonberry undergrowth rustled under her feet, and the grey, mossy outcrops sighed around her:

"Lisalill, Lisalill, where is your sweetheart?"

Lisalill rightly thought this to be going too far. She stood up as tall as she could, and shouted in vexation to all sides:

"Listen to the dumb forest! Listen to the silly hills! Tuwhit tuwhoo, I don't care for you!"

At last, she came to her grandfather in the skiff.

"Oh Grandpa," she said, "Now I have broken our jug and I have no water for you, Grandpa!"

"Yes, so I see," the old man grumbled. "That can happen when you send a child on an errand. But, my dear girl, why have you taken so long?"

Lisalill told him what she had heard in the forest.

"Do not worry about it," said grandfather. "It's just tittle-tattle among the trees, when the branches knock against each other, and that means we will get rain tomorrow. A sweetheart, what kind of foolish talk is that?"

"Yes, but I do have one," said Lisalill.

"You have the pussycat!"

"Then there are two, Grandpa. For you are the other."

"Well, that may be so. But now take our little empty butter tub, and go again to fetch me some water, for I am extremely thirsty."

Lisalill took the butter tub and began to walk again through the forest, and it was so, so quiet, that it was almost too quiet.

'I don't even hear a siskin[3] chirp,' Lisalill thought to herself. But the birds remained silent, and so Lisalill came upon a dog-rose bush, whose first flowers had just bloomed. Oh, they gave off a wonderful scent!

Lisalill plucked a flower to give to her grandfather, but there was something written on the leaves, and when she began to read the words, she saw it was the same question:

"Why do you walk all alone, Lisalill? Where is your sweetheart?"

"So, you're also posing that sappy query?" said Lisalill and threw away the flower. "I cannot understand what has come over the forest. Does it have nothing better to think about?"

So, she continued her quest for water, but found no spring. Instead, she found what she was not looking for, namely, all the rocks and bushes inscribed with that endless, tiresome question:

"Why do you walk all alone, Lisalill? Where is your sweetheart?"

"No, now the forest has gone completely crazy. I have to close my eyes," Lisalill said. And so she narrowed her eyelids as much as she could, but she had to squint a little every now and then so as not to stumble on the stones. At last, she came back to the shore without finding any water to scoop up in her grandfather's tub. She was about to return to the skiff, when she noticed a deep cleft in a large rock, on the side towards the sea, and in this gap there was still rainwater, for it had been in the shade.

Lisalill felt quite relieved and climbed as far as she could up onto the steep rock to reach the cleft. But when she reached down with the tub, she was close to falling, and the tub slipped out of her hand and rolled down into the sea. A gust of wind sped up, got hold of the tub and took it from the shore out to the open sea. Goodbye, butter tub!

"Oh, look at that," said Lisalill. "I'm back in the same mess. Now what shall I use to fetch water for Grandpa?"

And so, she sat down on the large rock and began to cry so bitterly that the tears fell like crowberries into the blue sea. But then she thought: 'How is it worthwhile to sit here and cry, when Grandpa is thirsty and waiting in the skiff? I will make a cup of birch bark and fetch him water from the crevice.'

No sooner said than done. She made a birch bark cup and began to clamber over the rock again. Then she happened to look down into the water and saw something glistening there. Lisalill became curious, hoisted up her dress, stepped into the water and stretched out her arm for the gleaming object. Though it was deep, she quickly held in her hand a beautiful bowl of the finest silver.

****

The Sea King sat in his sea-green hall, and all his court stood silent around him. The king's brow was overcast; he missed his youngest daughter, the water nymph Undine Marina, whom he had sent to pick corals from Australia's Barrier Reef. Undine Marina, as usual, played on the remote shore and left her footprints on the white sand. The young prince of the forest, who was her sweetheart, threw roses and daffodils at her in the roaring waves, and Undine Marina gathered them up. So time passed; Undine Marina playfully threw the regal shell, in which she should pick the corals, to the prince and the prince retained the shell. Then Undine Marina remembered her father's command and dived down to the depths to fetch a new shell from the royal castle. Meanwhile, one of the sea-trolls speculated to the king, saying:

"Undine Marina has neglected her mission and given her sweetheart a regal shell."

The Sea King became quite angry, for there was a war between him and the Forest King. But, keeping his anger hidden, he said to the troll:

"Get my silver bowl!"

The troll fetched the bowl, and it was very strangely made; everyone who drank from it would forget that which was most dear to them in life.

Undine Marina floated like a silver wave into the green palace and curtsied to her father.

"Where have you been all this time?" asked the Sea King. The princess replied:

"I've been frolicking on the sand, playing catch with flowers. But the forest prince took my shell, and now I have come to get a new one."

"Disobedient child," scolded the king. "I will let it go this time, but do not do it again! Look here, take my silver bowl instead of the shell, and fetch me cool, fresh water from some spring in the north, for I am tired of constantly drinking the salty seawater." The king thought to himself: 'My daughter will drink from the bowl and forget the young prince forever.'

Undine Marina took the bowl and floated away far over the sparkling sea, until she found a spring on the shore of Elgö island. There she filled the bowl with water from the spring, brought it to her petite red lips and drank, for she too had become thirsty in the summer heat. At that moment she forgot who she had loved most dearly in the whole world, and that was the young forest prince. But he had grown so firmly in her heart that she at once forgot everything else and floated away heedlessly with all the other thousand thoughtless waves crashing over each other in the boundless ocean.

****

So that's how Undine Marina's silver bowl came to lie on the white sand by Elgö's shore, and there it was found by Lisalill just when she was fetching water for her thirsty grandfather. Lisalill turned the bowl over and over with great astonishment, understanding nothing of its power but that it was strange and magnificent. 'It will be grand to fetch water for Grandpa in such a bowl,' she thought to herself.

Straightaway, she filled the bowl with water from the cleft in the rock. Oh, how that water sparkled cool and clear; it shone like the brightest silver. Lisalill could not resist the urge to taste it and drank ...

At that moment, she felt the blood flowing in her veins become like streams of ice. It became so wonderfully cool and quiet inside her. All the curious thoughts that had whirred around in her childish head suddenly fell from flight like shot birds, and there Lisalill sat as in a dream, no longer remembering the forest chatter or her grandfather in the boat, the grandfather whom she had loved best in all the world.

How long she sat there, no one knows, but it must have been long enough, for she had time to grew into a tall girl. The birds of the forest chirped as before, and the trees spoke both foolish and wise words, but Lisalill did not hear them. What would you care about things foolish or wise, when you do not have anyone in this world you care about?

Many rowed past and got to drink from Undine Marina's silver bowl, so Lisalill could do some good; 'Why else would I sit here?' she thought. Once there came a fisherwoman who had been crying for twenty years since her old man disappeared into the sea, she drank a deep draught from Undine Marina's silver bowl and cried no more. Another time, there came a vain girl, who never thought of anything but combing her beautiful hair, and when she drank, she dropped the comb into the sea. And yet another time, a gentleman sat there and fished; he loved nothing in the world as much as himself, and when he drank, he remembered how he lived well every day while his poor mother and sister froze and starved. Alas, how many would have to drink from Undine Marina's bowl all the way to the bottom so as to forget themselves!

Blind grandfather was neglected. Maybe he was still sitting in the skiff waiting for the precious water, which never seemed to come and quench his thirst.

One day a young sailor came to the shore of Elgö to cut wood for oars. He saw Lisalill sitting alone on the rock outcrop, and it occurred to him to jest and say:

"Why are you sitting all alone, Lisalill? Where is your sweetheart?"

Lisalill looked up, and she knew the sailor very well since they had played together before, when they were small. She looked at him, he looked at her, and at once the whole forest began to chirp. All the trees and branches, all the bushes and leaves, all the rocks and hummocks were at once full again with the same incomprehensible words, which before would have so earnestly teased and annoyed Lisalill when she went to look for the spring on Elgö.

"Oh no, Grandpa is still waiting in the skiff!" exclaimed Lisalill, and at once she jumped up and ran with such haste over stumps and stones that half of the water tipped out of Undine Marina's silver bowl.

"Look at that!" said the sailor, and at that moment he cut the axe into a stone, so that a large piece flew out of the blade.

Lisalill ran as fast as she could, and would you believe it, there sat the grandfather still waiting in the skiff.

"Where have you been all this time?" he scolded.

Lisalill spoke about what had happened and how she had found the silver bowl, but she did not say a single word about the sailor, for she had completely forgotten that such a sailor existed. And the moment she forgot him, she remembered her grandfather.

"Now you must drink, Grandpa!" she exclaimed, holding the bowl to the old man's lips. Grandfather drank and forgot, like all the others, what he held most dear in the world; that was the light in his eyes. He now found it perfectly fine to be blind, and no longer remembered that he had ever seen the sun, the moon, the stars, the blue lake, and the green forest.

Meanwhile, the Sea King sat in his sea-green castle, waiting in vain for his daughter to return. Then he sent out the sea troll, to seek her out, but the troll returned with the message that Undine Marina had forgotten everything and floated like a thoughtless wave on the wide ocean. The king became angry and turned the sea troll into a reef in the Gulf of Finland: many ships now sink there in the autumn storms. But that did not bring his daughter back. She disappeared, and with the loss and longing, the sea king's beard became silver-grey.

Lisalill rowed home with her grandfather, and everything was as before. Grandfather mended other fishermen's nets and Lisalill made birch-twig brushes and put out the nets in the evening. So they still do to this day. But Undine Marina's silver bowl was sold to the silversmith, and who can say where it has ended up? Maybe someone has bought it to use as a cream jug for the coffee table and is now wondering how everyone who drinks from it soon forgets what was most dear to them in the whole world.

Sometimes the young sailor comes rowing to the shore at Lisalill's cottage and looks up sadly at the small window. But Lisalill does not know him: she ties the birch twigs together and listens to the trees singing outside:

"Why are you so lonely, Lisalill? Where is your sweetheart?"

"Yes, who knows," responds Lisalill, wanting so badly to laugh at the thought, but she cannot. There is still something sad and strange that she does not really understand.

Oh, you little golden bird, that sings so beautifully in the blue sky, sing once more the same words for Lisalill, and sing them for Undine Marina's wave in the open sea! Maybe they will hear you, maybe they will get their memory back. Sing for the thoughtless wave:

"Undine Marina, Undine Marina, do you no longer remember your friend in the forest?"

Then sing your song for the girl in the cabin once again:

"Lisalill, Lisalill, why are you so alone, and where is your sweetheart?"

Ride a Cockhorse

There is a nursery rhyme that everyone knows but few understand: it is a game that everyone sings, but no one sings the song through to the end. It was sung by my grandmother when she was little, and it was heard by my grandfather when he was very young. Yesterday our old nurse-maid Dora sang the same song for our two-year-old boy. And when she sang, the little boy rode on her knee like a man in the saddle, and the horse ran and did not budge, and the rider rode and never arrived. But the song was not like the songs of today; it was a song from old times, it was funny, it was sad, there was the clash of swords in its tones, there was the babbling of a child's voice. And as they sang, I became weak at heart; the more I heard, the more I listened. I hugged our old Dora and asked her to sing that song again. Then Dora smiled, and said, "There's more to it than the tune one sings, there's more to it than the children who babble. Past times live on in it, and if you want to hear it, I can sing it for you. Pay attention, now my song starts again."

"Rida, rida ranka" "Ride a cockhorse"

More than five hundred years ago, there was a prince called Haakon[1]. He was eight years old, beautiful and light-hearted, with the mildest blue eyes and soft cheeks, red as apples. His father, King Magnus[2], ruled over all the kingdom of Sweden and Finland, with their mountains and forests, lakes and seas, towns and villages. He commanded many ships and brave armies, proud knights, shiny swords, warhorses, bows, lances and glittering armour. There were many elegant ladies and charming maidens in the king's court, but none prouder and more beautiful than the king's consort, Queen Blanca[3], the mother of little

Prince Haakon. One day she sat in her purple-draped chambers in the royal castle, holding the little prince in her arms. He rode on her knee, as a child often does, and the beautiful queen sang:

"Rida, rida ranka" "Ride a cockhorse"

"hästen heter Blanca" "Horsey is called Blanca"

It was gracious for such a proud queen to want to be a horse for her dearest little boy. The prince liked to ride. He had often delighted in seeing the knights and squires directing their snorting steeds in the courtyard and galloping out through the gate, sparks flying. He had been sitting in the high seats of honour next to his mother last summer, when the big jousting tournament was held out on the list field. There, the counts and dukes had ridden against each other with long lances ... the trumpets clattered, the feathered plumes swayed, the horses neighed, and in clouds of dust, the knights tumbled over each other in the wide, flag-decorated field. Prince Haakon could not forget this; he had so often dreamed that one day he, too, would sit in the saddle with a sword, armour and spurs, like other kings' sons. Oh, how he would then ride far and wide, around the world, to exploits and adventures! So, as he now rode on his mother's knee, his beautiful eyes began to twinkle; and when mother sang:

"Rida, rida ranka" "Ride a cockhorse"

"hästen heter Blanca" "Horsey is called Blanca"

the boy, in his childish voice, asked:

"Vart ska vi ria?" "Where are we going?"

That was quite a question! Perhaps he was waiting for his mother to answer: 'away to the tournament', or 'off to the Holy Land', where so many brave heroes had ridden before, though few had returned. Or was it his intention to ride away to the deep forests of Finland, where his great-great-grandfather, the great Birger Jarl[4], had previously fought against trolls and pagans? But his mother, the queen, had other thoughts; she was a wise queen, and she pondered how the little prince might one day win new kingdoms and lands without the clash of swords. Therefore, when the boy asked:

"Vart ska vi ria?"	"Where are we going?"

his mother kissed his forehead and sang:

"Ria bort och fria"	"Ride forth and pay court"
"till en liten pia."	"To a fair maiden"

There was a particular girl that the queen was thinking of, and she was still lying in her cradle. But she was certainly a bride to consider, for she was not only a king's daughter, but also the heiress to a mighty kingdom. The queen knew this, but not the little prince, of course. And when his mother sang:

"Ria bort och fria"	"Ride forth and pay court"
"till en liten pia."	"To a fair maiden"

the boy asked:

"Vad skall hon heta?"	"What is her name?"

Yes, this was still a big secret. The queen did not wish to reveal it to all the world - not to any chamberlain, monk or knight, not even to the king, her spouse. For her plans were nothing less than the acquisition of a kingdom, and such a scheme must not be revealed to any gossipy tongues. It would be difficult to win such a bride; there would certainly be no lack of suitors from east and west. Yet, when the prince so innocently asked:

"Vad skall hon heta?"	"What is her name?"

The queen, unable to resist her mother's heart, bowed the prince's curly head down into her bosom, placed both hands around his eyes, and whispered:

"Jungfru Margareta" "Princess Margareta"

So that was it. Princess Margareta[5] was the daughter and heir to the throne of the Danish king Valdemar. Prince Haakon would one day win her as a bride and with her, the kingdom of Denmark. With this song, the wise queen Blanca wanted to plant this shrewd idea for the future into the boy's heart while he was still small, so that he would accomplish it when he grew up. Prince Haakon would one day carry on his head all the crowns of Sweden, Norway and Denmark. She kissed the boy once more and whispered again, half-jokingly, half seriously:

"Jungfru Margareta" "Princess Margareta"

Just then, King Magnus entered the queen's bower, and behind him followed two ladies-in-waiting who served the Queen. The king enjoyed beautiful songs, and he loved to hear the queen sing. When outside, he had heard the song but not the words, so he asked what the queen was singing.

Queen Blanca, as has been noted, had no desire to reveal her future plans to the king, who was not very discreet, let alone to the maids. She replied that it was only childish nonsense that she sang for her little boy.

"Sing it again," 'said the king. "I fancy it is a pretty song."

"It's a silly little song," said the queen. "It is about a young knight's courtship of a maid of honour, and it goes well in the beginning, but ends badly."

"Well, sing!" said the king.

The queen sang:

"When he came to the king's court,
there was no one at home,
only an old woman ..."

"That must have been quite annoying for the young knight," the king exclaimed. "Well, what did the old dragon who guarded the courtyard do?"

"Sat in the corner,
Dressed the distaff with flax
and taught her daughter to spin."

"So, there was also a young lady at home. Well, go on; what happened next?" asked the king.

"Spin, spin, my daughter!
Tomorrow your fiancé will come."

King Magnus laughed. "What do you know! The old woman wanted to cheer up her daughter so that the work would not be so tedious. And then?"

"Her daughter, she spun,
and the tears flowed ..."

"Poor little thing!"

"But that fiancé never showed up ..."

"That was very tender and touching," said the king. "Well, he never arrived?"

"Until the second year,
with gold ribbon in his hair ..."

"I am glad for that," said the king. "Otherwise, it would have been too distressing. Well, that's how it turned out, the young knight found his sweetheart."

"But no-one understands why …"

sang the Queen, and that was how the song ended.

"What do you mean by that, my dearest queen?" asked the king. "I thought the romance was very clear and straightforward."

"My lord and king," replied Queen Blanca, "It is usually the case in romances that there is something left to the imagination. And that's precisely the beauty of it."

"No doubt!" said the king. "One could imagine that there was a splendid wedding. Thanks for the song; it was really cheerful. And now I want to take my little Haakon away with me. He should be taught to ride real horses, rather than his mother's knee. Do you want to come with me to the stable yard, little boy?"

"Yes, please," said the boy. With a jump he was in his father's arms and quickly forgot both the maiden Margareta and the whole song.

~~~~~~~~~~~~~~~~~~~~~~~~~~~~~~~~~~~~

Time passed and the infant Margareta, King Valdemar's daughter, grew up in her father's court in Denmark and became a prudent princess with quick, dark eyes and a happy disposition. When she was six years old, she already had many suitors, who probably thought more about the Danish crown than about the little princess. What used to be a secret was no more, for knights and counsellors came from the Swedish royal castle to the Danish one to negotiate a union between the two royal children. The engagement was first settled, then abandoned, then agreed again. At the age of ten, Princess Margareta herself hardly knew if she were engaged or not; the exalted courtiers would not bother to consult an adult fiancée; why then inform a child? It amused
~~~~~~~~~~~~~~~~~~~~~~~~~~~~~~~~~~~~

little Princess Margareta to be so sought after, but she thought it was even more amusing to pull the beards of the old counsellors when they sought an audience with her father on wooing business. And for that the princess was punished by her strict governess, Lady Martha[6]; in those days, even princes and princesses were punished when they were naughty.

One beautiful summer morning, when Princess Margareta was eleven years old, she went out with her childhood friend, Ingegerd Knutsdotter[7], to play in the park close to her father's castle, down by the seashore. White sails could be seen out to sea, and the two children had fun skimming flat stones across the water.

"Now let's play a game," said Princess Margareta. "I will throw a stone for each of my suitors, and I will embrace the one that bounces the most."

"That will take a lot of stones" said the maiden Ingegerd. "I hope that Prince Haakon of Sweden and Norway gets the most bounces."

"We'll all get to see how good he is," said the princess, laughing. "Now I'm throwing the Count of Mecklenburg. Splash, he just sank, he is scratched straightway. Who do we have next?

"The Margrave of Brandenburg."

"Splish-splash! The Margrave of Brandenburg made one bounce. That doesn't satisfy me. Who do we have next?"

"The Duke of Holstein."

"Let's go for the Duke with his red hair. Splish-splash, three bounces! I may have to think about becoming a duchess. Who is next?"

"The Count of Flanders."

"Splash! Flanders went to the bottom. Do we have more?"

"The Prince of Saxony."

"He, who has half his nose split by a sword blow? Splish-splash! He made four bounces. It's over now, Ingegerd. No one can manage more than four bounces."

"Try one more; maybe there's another winner." And Ingegerd chose a fine, flat stone, good for skimming.

"Never believe that Prince Haakon will get even a little finger from me," said Princess Margareta. She laughed, turned about on her red high heels and carelessly threw the stone without even looking at it. But Haakon made six bounces.

"Oh!" shouted both girls.

At the same moment, the foliage rustled, and a young, handsome knight came riding into the park, accompanied by squires dressed in gold and scarlet. His armour gleamed in the sun, and the white feathers on his helmet swayed in the light summer breeze. With a leap he was off his horse, strode towards the two girls, bowed a knee to Princess Margareta, and said:

"Dearest maiden, I have come here, over land and sea, to bring you my chivalrous tribute. I am Prince Haakon, and with your exalted Father's consent, I lay the crowns of Sweden and Norway at your feet."

Princess Margareta blushed at these words, as if she had been sixteen years old. But since she was still only eleven, she soon took courage and said:

"Are you the one who made six bounces?"

Prince Haakon truly did not know how to answer such an odd question from his intended royal bride; but when he observed by her sparkling eyes that she was not at all as eccentric as she seemed, he said:

"Not only six bounces, noble maiden, but six crowns I would wish to offer you if you deign to allow me to attach this ring to your finger." And with these words he pressed a diamond ring of great value onto his bride-to-be's ring finger.

Princess Margareta willingly let this happen, for she rightly thought that the young prince was the most handsome and accomplished groom she could wish for. But she did not want to give herself away so easily. She removed the ring from her finger again, pretended to look at it carefully and said:

"Are these stones glass?"

"No, noble maiden," said the prince. "It's a diamond from India."

""I wish it were a granite stone, so I could try my luck again," said the maiden. At once she turned and threw the ring as far as she could into the sea. "You see," she said. "It didn't bounce even once!"

"That is because it was so reluctant to be parted from your finger," replied the prince, without showing any displeasure. But he continued, "If you will allow, I would like to try this." Whereupon he loosened a large gold medal, which he carried on a chain over his cuirass, and threw it forcefully out over the shiny surface of the sea. The heavy gold coin made jump after jump before it finally disappeared under the water, and one could count eight bounces.

Then Princess Margareta reached out her hand to Prince Haakon and said:

"You're not throwing badly! Next time we will throw with crowns."

A few weeks later, Prince Haakon was married to Princess Margareta. It was a magnificent wedding, celebrated throughout the Danish kingdom with tournaments, dances, free-flowing wine and roasted oxen. But on the wedding night, the bride was chastised by Lady

Martha (her governess) because she bit the groom when he wanted to kiss her.

Sometime later, Princess Margareta was sent with Prince Haakon to Norway to become its queen. Lady Martha followed and continued to discipline the queen. This must have been worthwhile, for when Queen Margareta grew up and gained more understanding, she became the most wise and judicious queen that ever wore a crown in the north.

Eight years after the wedding, Queen Margareta was blessed with a little prince, named Olof[8]. He was genial and blue-eyed; he also greatly enjoyed riding. One day Prince Olof sat on his mother's knee, and she sang to him a Danish song about how the knight Nils Ebbesen killed the scourge of the peasants, Count Gert. But Queen Margareta's singing was rough and not as beautiful as Queen Blanca's.

King Haakon came in and listened to the song for a while. Then his own mother's riding song ran through his mind, and he took the boy on his knee. "You should sing," said the Queen. "My voice is gruffer than yours."

King Haakon sang:

"Rida, rida ranka"	"Ride a cockhorse"
"hästen heter Blanca"	"Horsey is called Blanca"

"That was your mother," said the queen.

"Yes," said the king, and continued to sing.

"Vart ska vi ria?"	"Where are we going?"
"Ria bort och fria"	"Ride forth and pay court"
"till en liten pia."	"To a fair maiden"
"Vad skall hon heta?"	"What is her name?"
"Jungfru Margareta"	"Princess Margareta"

"That was me," said the queen.

"I do not know if you will understand the rest of the song," said the king, "because it was sung to obscure the beginning."

> "When we came to the king's court,
>
> there was no one at home,
>
> only an old woman ..."

"Well, you can skip that," said the queen. "How did it end?"

> "That fiancé never showed up ..."

"He came eventually," said Queen Margareta. "Yes, he came in the end," said King Haakon.

And then both the king and the queen smiled. The little prince Olof rode around the world on his father's knee, just as his father had ridden on his mother's knee. We could say much more about them all but that is probably enough said about the song. Every child today still knows that song, but not everyone knows about whom it was first sung. The little boy who rides a cockhorse today no longer knows about Prince Haakon, who rode out courting, and the little girl who sings for her doll about maiden Margareta no longer knows who the song's Princess was. Kings, queens, princes and princesses die, as everyone does; but beautiful and happy songs do not die: their melodies ride proudly from generation to generation.

Notes

The Weathercock

'Kyrktuppen'. From Läsning för Barn, Första Boken; A. Bonniers Förlag, Stockholm, 1906 and Topelius Sagor 1; H. Schildts Förlag, Helsingfors 1953.

1. Topelius refers to Gilimiliadolgas.

Original Prologue: Now we start with a remarkable story, which could be called 'Pride comes before a fall', but everyone is free to make up their own mind. You can be self-important even if you are never anything more than a worm in a raspberry; what then when one has the honor of being a church weathercock!

The Old Cottage

'Gamla Stugan'. From Läsning för Barn, Första Boken; A. Bonniers Förlag, Stockholm, 1906 and Topelius Sagor 1; H. Schildts Förlag, Helsingfors 1953.

1. According to tradition, the tomte lived in the houses and barns of a farmstead and secretly acted as their guardian. If treated well, he protected the family and animals from evil and misfortune and helped with the chores and farm work. The tomte was usually imagined as a small, elderly man, often with a full white beard and wearing a red conical or knit cap.

2. A fish - Perca fluviatilis.

3. Arctic bramble/raspberry - Rubus arcticus.

4. Topelius mentions Fjäderholmarna (the Feather Isles), imaginary islands in the Finnish archipelago.

The Feather Isles

'Fjäderholmarna'. From Läsning för Barn, Första Boken; A. Bonniers Förlag, Stockholm, 1906.

1. Topelius names her Signora Mara.

2. Topelius names him Nukku Matti.

Forest Bear

'Skogsbjörn'. From Läsning för Barn, Svenska litteratursällskapet i Finland, Helsingfors 2021 and Topelius Sagor 1; H. Schildts Förlag, Helsingfors 1953.

1. Topelius uses the name Guldberg and calls his son Moses. The names have been changed to the Russian Kovalyov (see Gogol) and his son Moisey.

2. Also means bear, hence his nickname.

3. A jolly boat and a pinnace were small rowing boats carried by a ship in the age of sail.

4. Topelius names him Nukku Matti, and says the Swedes call him John Blund and the Danes (see HC Anderson) Ole Luköje.

5. One thousand riksdaler was equivalent to 3.6 years of wages for the average Swedish male worker in 1860, equivalent to US$189,000 in 2015.

6. Cod pickled with lye.

Knut Spelevink

'Knut Spelevink'. From Läsning för Barn, Svenska litteratursällskapet i Finland, Helsingfors 2021 and Topelius Sagor 2; H. Schildts Förlag, Helsingfors 1953.

1. A water nymph and underwater princess - see later story.

2. A double meaning, since 'spela' can mean play music or play tricks. 'Spelevink' can mean 'irresponsible youth' or 'prankster'.

3. In the mid-19th Century, in the Lutheran Church of Sweden and Finland, there was an annual assessment of parishioners' biblical knowledge using the book 'Martin Luther's little catechism'. For example, the pastor would ask: "The ninth commandment - What is that?" And the parishioners would give their learnt response.

4. Topelius uses the Swedish word 'lakrom' which in English means roe (eggs) of a burbot (a fish).

Wipplustig

'Wipplustig'. From Läsning för Barn, Svenska litteratursällskapet i Finland, Helsingfors 2021 and Topelius Sagor 2; H. Schildts Förlag, Helsingfors 1953.

1. Lustig can mean comic or strange, or both. (Like funny - haha or peculiar).

Little Lasse

'Lasse liten'. From Läsning för Barn, Första Boken; A. Bonniers Förlag, Stockholm, 1906 and Topelius Sagor 2; H. Schildts Förlag, Helsingfors 1953.

1. Topelius refers to the old man Nukku Matti (see the story about the Feather Isles).

2. Topelius refers to Fjäderholmarna (the Feather Isles), imaginary islands in the Finnish archipelago.

3. Swedish word for sauna (Finnish).

4. Topelius writes 'Fortunate are they that God holds dear'.

Translator's comment: Given our current sensitivities about racial stereotypes, note that it is a Nordic writer (and translator) making references to skin colour in the different continents. One could bear in mind that in the story it is a child's perspective, in a dream, and written in the 1860s so stereotypes are unsurprising. Nothing negative is said about the different people and their colours, the things Lasse fears are the natural wildlife – dogs, tigers, snakes etc. I see the story as noticing diversity around the world and saying, in the song, that they are 'Happy that God loves them all'.

A Winter's Tale about Skyhigh and Cloudbeard

'Vintersagan om Skyhög och Molnskägg'. From Läsning för Barn, Svenska litteratursällskapet i Finland, Helsingfors 2021 and Topelius Sagor 2; H. Schildts Förlag, Helsingfors 1953.

1. The light inner bark of the pine tree is harvested in the spring. It is kept outside in the open air until it hardens like cardboard. Then it could be ground into a flour or roasted in an oven until light brown, like a flatbread. Pine bark served as famine food in Finland, most recently during the famine of 1866-1868 and during and after the civil war of 1918.

2. A bird - Lagopus lagopus.

3. A broom made of twigs.

Sampo Lappelill

'Sampo Lappelill'. From Läsning för Barn, Tredje Boken; A. Bonniers Förlag, Stockholm, 1906 and Topelius Sagor 2; H. Schildts Förlag, Helsingfors 1953.

1. Topelius describes Lapland and the Lapps. Nowadays, these people refer to themselves as Sámi and their homeland as Sámpi. In 1860, they were mostly nomadic, following their reindeer herds.

2. Sleigh shaped like the front half of a canoe.

3. Tenojoki in Finnish.

4. See the Kalevala for more on Sampo, and on Hiisi.

5. Literally 'little Lapp', but in this story, Sampo Lappelill is heroic.

The Waterlily

'Neckrosen'. From Läsning för Barn, Svenska litteratursällskapet i Finland, Helsingfors 2021 and Topelius Sagor 2; H. Schildts Förlag, Helsingfors 1953.

1. A fish - Gymnocephalus cernua.

2. A water-sprite.

Adlamina's Pearl

'Adalminas perla'. From Läsning för Barn, Svenska litteratursällskapet i Finland, Helsingfors 2021 and Topelius Sagor 2; H. Schildts Förlag, Helsingfors 1953.

1. Topelius adds here: 'held her so dear that it was almost too much, for God does not like one to love someone with an idolatrous passion. Then one forgets what is written in the catechism, that one should love God with all one's heart and with all one's soul.'

2. Topelius writes this phrase as: 'according to God's will'.

The Water Nymph's Footsteps

'Unda Marinas fotspår' From Läsning för Barn, Svenska litteratursällskapet i Finland, Helsingfors 2021 and Topelius Sagor 3; H. Schildts Förlag, Helsingfors 1953.

1. Topelius writes 'behold the goodness of God'.

Roaring Waters and Sighing Streams

'Brusebäck och Susebäck' From Läsning för Barn, Svenska litteratursällskapet i Finland, Helsingfors 2021 and Topelius Sagor 3; H. Schildts Förlag, Helsingfors 1953.

1. Topelius writes 'the good God'.

2. Topelius writes 'Therefore grant that we may seek our greatness, our power, our eternal purpose in You alone, our Lord and God. May we early on tame our proud minds with humility and then become good, blessed children for your kingdom in heaven and your kingdom on earth!'

3. Topelius writes 'always remembered God's good intentions with the images in abundant Nature that He reveals to the human gaze.'

Translator's note: Compare the images of watery oblivion in this story with 'The Dewdrop slips into the shining sea', the final words of Edward Arnold's epic poem The Light of Asia (first published in 1879), based on the philosophy of Buddhism.

Raspberry Masquerade

'Hallonmasken'. From Läsning för Barn, Tredje Boken; A. Bonniers Förlag, Stockholm, 1906 and Topelius Sagor 3; H. Schildts Förlag, Helsingfors 1953.

1. Larva of the Raspberry beetle (Byturus tomentosus). The Swedish word for larva is 'mask', hence the pun in the English title of this story.

2. Fruit of the dwarf cornel - Cornus suecica.

Christmas with the Trolls

'Trollens Jul'. From Läsning för Barn, Fjärde Boken; A. Bonniers Förlag, Stockholm, 1906 and Topelius Sagor 3; H. Schildts Förlag, Helsingfors 1953.

1. One edition of the story mentions the visit of the 'julbocken', the Yule goat.

2. See the Sampo Lappelill story.

3. Scissors for trimming the wick of a candle.

The Sea King's Gift

'Havskonungens gåva'. From Läsning för Barn, Svenska litteratursällskapet i Finland, Helsingfors 2021 and Topelius Sagor 3; H. Schildts Förlag, Helsingfors 1953.

1. A firkin is a small barrel.

2. Small-beer, around 2% alcohol and in olden days, safer to drink than water.

3. Buckling is a hot-smoked herring (a kipper is cold-smoked).

4. A collection of verses about ancient Finnish gods and heroes.

5. A water sprite.

6. A restorative remedy for hair, popular in the 1800s.

<u>Bullerbasius</u>

'Bullerbasius'. From Läsning för Barn, Femte Boken; A. Bonniers Förlag, Stockholm, 1906 and Topelius Sagor 4; H. Schildts Förlag, Helsingfors 1953.

1. In those days, every family baked bread for their own needs and used a wooden (oak) dough trough for fermenting rye flour dough.

2. The leader of the herd, with a cowbell around its neck.

<u>The Water Nymph's Silver Bowl</u>

'Unda Marinas silverskål'. From Läsning för Barn, Fjärde Boken; A. Bonniers Förlag, Stockholm, 1906 and Topelius Sagor 4; H. Schildts Förlag, Helsingfors 1953.

1. Between the islands of Skåldö and Elgö in the Ekenäs archipelago, Finland.

2. A bird - Tetrastes bonasia.

3. A bird - Spinus spinus.

<u>Ride a Cockhorse</u>

'Rida Ranka'. From Läsning för Barn, Femte Boken; A. Bonniers Förlag, Stockholm, 1906 and Topelius Sagor 4; H. Schildts Förlag, Helsingfors 1953.

1. Haakon VI (1340-80), King of Norway 1343-80, King of Sweden 1362-64.

2. Magnus IV (1316-74), King of Sweden 1319-64.

3. Blanche of Namur (1320-63), married Magnus IV 1336.

4. Birger (1210-1266) led the Second Swedish Crusade which established Swedish rule in Finland.

5. Princess Margareta (1353-1412), daughter of Valdemar IV of Denmark, married Haakon VI 1363, Queen of Norway and Denmark 1387-1412, Queen of Sweden 1389-1412.

6. Olaf II (1370-87), King of Denmark 1376-87, King of Norway 1380-87.

7. Margareta "Märta" Ulfsdotter (1319-1371).

8. Ingegerd Knutsdotter (1356-1412) was daughter of Märta Ulfsdotter.

Zacharias Topelius (1818 – 1898) was a Swedish-speaking Finnish author, professor, journalist, and poet. In 1841, he worked as the editor of Helsinki Newspapers. In 1854 he was appointed professor of history at the University of Helsinki and was rector of the University before his retirement in 1878. He wrote and published many tales, poems and plays for children over a period of almost fifty years (1847-1896). This volume offers a small selection.

Paul Gustav Whittaker, DPhil, FRSM, was born in Finland and grew up in England. For 20 years, he worked as a Clinical Scientist at Newcastle University's Medical School. In 1998, he relocated to Philadelphia, PA, USA and was a researcher in women's health for a further 20 years. He continues to be inspired by the sights and sounds of lake and sea, the rhythms and cadences of world music and by those striving for social justice.